The
French Classical Romances

Complete in Twenty Crown Octavo Volumes

Editor-in-Chief
EDMUND GOSSE, LL.D.

With Critical Introductions and Interpretative Essays by

HENRY JAMES   PROF. RICHARD BURTON   HENRY HARLAND

ANDREW LANG   PROF. F. C. DE SUMICHRAST

THE EARL OF CREWE   HIS EXCELLENCY M. CAMBON

PROF. WM. P. TRENT   ARTHUR SYMONS   MAURICE HEWLETT

DR. JAMES FITZMAURICE-KELLY   RICHARD MANSFIELD

BOOTH TARKINGTON   DR. RICHARD GARNETT

PROF. WILLIAM M. SLOANE   JOHN OLIVER HOBBES

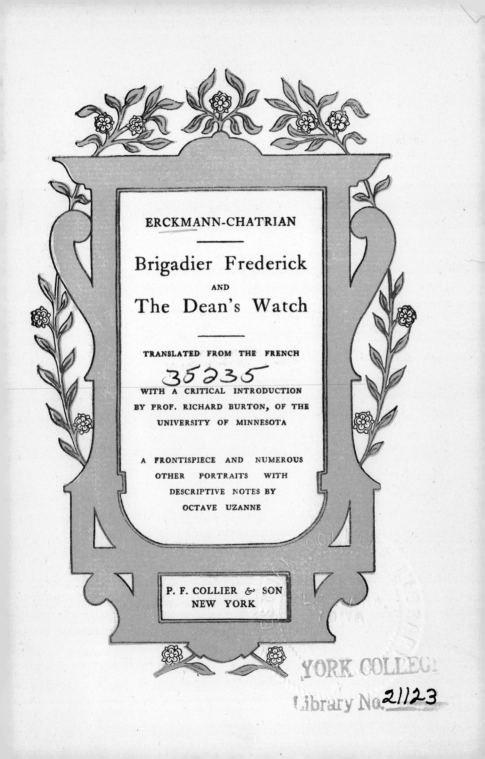

ERCKMANN-CHATRIAN

Brigadier Frederick

AND

The Dean's Watch

TRANSLATED FROM THE FRENCH

35235

WITH A CRITICAL INTRODUCTION
BY PROF. RICHARD BURTON, OF THE
UNIVERSITY OF MINNESOTA

A FRONTISPIECE AND NUMEROUS
OTHER PORTRAITS WITH
DESCRIPTIVE NOTES BY
OCTAVE UZANNE

P. F. COLLIER & SON
NEW YORK

ERCKMANN–CHATRIAN

FASHIONS change in literature, but certain
things abide. There may be disputes from generation to generation, even from decade to decade,
as to what is æsthetic, or what is beautiful; there
is less as to what is human. The work of the
French writers, whose duality is quite lost in the
long-time association of their names for the purposes of story making, seems at the least to make
this claim to outlast its authors: it is delightfully
saturated with humanity.

And this humanity is of the sort that, since it
can be understood of all men, is therefore very
widely acceptable. It is well to emphasize the
point in an attempt to explain the popularity of
Erckmann-Chatrian, immediate or remote. There
are other reasons, to be sure: but this one is at
the door, knocking to be heard. But to speak of
the essential humanity of these books is not to
deny or ignore their art; that they have in abundance—quite as truly indeed as the work of your

most insistent advocate of "art for art"; but it is
art for life's sake. In the best sense, the verisimilitude of the Erckmann-Chatrian stories is admirable, impressive. They are, as a rule, exquisitely in
key. They produce a cumulative effect by steadily,
unobtrusively clinging to a single view-point, that
of the speaker who is an eye-witness, and the result is a double charm—that of reality and that of
illusion. One sees life, not through the eyes of
the authors, but through the eyes of the characters;
hence the frequent setting-forth of principles is re-
lieved from didacticism by the careful way in which
the writers refrain from expressing their own opinion. So artistic are they that they even indulge in
the delicate ruse of opposing the views which are
really their own, thereby producing a still stronger
effect of fair-mindedness and detachment.

Yet, as the world knows, in the most justly
famed of their books, the so-called National
Novels, it is their purpose to preach against war;
they are early advocates of the principles of the
Peace Congress at The Hague, forerunners, in
their own fashion, of the ideas expressed in art
and literature by later men like Tolstoy and
Verestchagin.

The local colour—one still uses the phrase as
convenient—is remarkable for its sympathetic

fidelity; the style well-nigh a model of prose whose purpose it is to depict in homely yet picturesque terms the passage of great events, seen by humble, it may be Philistine, folk, and hence not seen *couleur de rose*. When a heartfelt sympathy for average human-kind rises to the surface of the author's feeling, some candid, cordial phrase is ever found to express it.

The work of Erckmann-Chatrian, voluminous as it is, can be easily classified : it mainly consists of the idyl and the picture of war ; *L'Illustre Docteur Mathéus*, their first success, happily illustrates the former *genre* ; any one of the half dozen tales making up the National Novel series may be taken to represent the latter. Both veins turned out to be gold mines, so rich were they in the free-milling ore of popular favour. Such stories as *L'Ami Fritz* and *The Brigadier Frederick* are types of the two kinds of fiction which panned out most richly also for the world. In the idyl dealing with homely provincial life—the life of their home province—these authors are, of a truth, masters. The story is naught, the way of telling it, all that breeds atmosphere and innuendo, is everything. In *L'Ami Fritz* the plot may be told in a sentence : 'tis the wooing and winning of a country lass, daughter of a farmer, by a well-to-do jovial bache-

Erckmann–Chatrian

lor of middle age in a small town; *voilà tout*; yet the tale makes not only delicious reading, it leaves a permanent impression of pleasure—one is fain to re-read it. It is rich in human nature, in a comfortable sense of the good things of the earth; food and drink, soft beds, one's seat at the tavern, spring sunlight, and the sound of a fiddle playing dance tunes at the fair : and, on a higher plane, of the genial joys of comradeship and the stanch belief in one's native land. When the subtler passion of love comes in upon this simple pastoral scene, the gradual discovery of Friend Fritz that the sentiment he has always ridiculed has him at last in its clutch, is portrayed with a sly unction, a kindly humour overlying an unmistakable tenderness of heart, which give the tale great charm. Sweetness and soundness are fundamentals of such literature.

This tale is a type of them all, though deservedly the best liked. Love of nature and of human nature, a knowledge of the little, significant things that make up life, an exquisite realism along with a sort of temperamental optimism which assumes good of men and women—these blend in the provincial stories in such a way that one's sense of art is charmed while in no less degree one's sense of life is quickened and com-

Erckmann–Chatrian

forted. Erckmann-Chatrian introduced to French readers the genuine Alsatian, not the puppet of the vaudeville stage. Their books are, among other things, historical documents. From their sketches and tales better than in any other way one can gain an understanding of the present German provinces of Alsace and Lorraine during a period stretching from the Revolution to and after the Franco-Prussian war. The Alsatian in their hands is seen distinctly as one of the most interesting of Gallic provincial types.

The attitude of Dr. Mathéus, that charming physician savant, who is in love with science, with the great world of scholarship and literary fame, and so is fain to leave his simple countryside in quest of renown—in his final return to his home as, after all, the best spot on earth, typifies the teaching of these authors in all their works. The tale is a sort of allegory, veiling a sermon on the value of the "fireside clime" of home hearths and hearts. Nor must it be forgotten that these writers cultivated the short story or tale with vigour and success; *The Dean's Watch*, printed in the present volume, is an excellent example of the *genre*. Erckmann-Chatrian, especially in the earlier years of their conjoined labour, wrote numerous pieces of short fiction which abounded in gruesome ad-

venture and situations more or less startling—
witness the Heidelberg murder story. They possessed a considerable talent for the detective fiction brought to a fine art by Poe and worthily
carried on in our day by Conan Doyle. Yet
even here the work has a higher value—perhaps
the highest—for the thoughtful reader in that it
affords a faithful transcript of German life in
time gone by; the authors, although so circum-
scribed in space, are in some sort historians of
piquant social conditions. It is commonly said
that your true short-story writer is not a novelist, nor the other way about. But *The Dean's
Watch*, and a dozen other tales that could be
named, are little master-pieces not to be omitted
in any just, comprehensive survey of these fecund
authors.

The National Novels differ from these simpler
tales in more than theme and the fuller body and
greater variety they possess; the authors' aim in
the series sets the books apart from the other
stories. This group is made up of tales that fairly
may be called "purpose fiction," in the present
cant. Erckmann-Chatrian agree to hate war and
to justify their hate by writing a succession of
books portraying its horrors, always from the dis-
advantage-point of actual humble participants and

onlookers, so that the plea shall appear to be at once fairly made and yet be overwhelming in effect. Of the result, surely it may be said of the National Novels that if they are not magnificent, they are war—war stript of its glory, reduced to the one grim denominator of human misery.

The successive national struggles of France towards that peaceful Republicanism which has now endured long enough to induce the outside world into a belief that this volatile, fiery people will never revert to any form of monarchy, are sketched so graphically as to give a clear comprehension of their history. Nowhere is the artistry of the authors better exhibited than in the skill with which, by placing their own position in the mouths of others and by means of their remarkable power in characterization, they rob special pleading of that didacticism which is so deadly an enemy of good fiction. To secure an effect of verisimilitude no method of story-telling is perhaps so useful as that in which one of the characters speaks in proper person. What the author loses in omniscience, he more than gains in the impression of reality. This method is admirable in the hands of Erckmann-Chatrian, who consistently use it in their fiction. Do the writers of any other nation, one is tempted to query, offer such frequent examples of good taste in this avoidance of the too didactic as do the French? In some English hands so strenuous an attempt would have seemed heavily intolerable. Here one forgets all but the naturalness of word and action in the characters; and the lesson sinks the deeper into the mind.

In justice both to our authors and the present-day temper, it may be declared that the Twentieth Century is likely to be more sympathetic to their particular thesis than was their own time. There is a popular treatment of war which bedecks it in a sort of stage tinsel, to the hiding of its gaunt figure and cadaverous face. Some of Scott's romances are of this order. Zola, with his epic sweep in *Le Débâcle*, does not disguise the horrors of the Franco-Prussian struggle. Yet epic it is, and in a sense, romantic; handled by a poet whose imagination is aroused by the magnitude and movement of his theme. Erckmann-Chatrian set themselves squarely against this conception; they reduce the splendid trappings and *elan* of battle to its true hideousness.

In order to depict the inevitable, wretched results of the killing of men for purposes of political ambition, or national aggrandizement, Erckmann-Chatrian, as in their provincial idyls, cling steadily to the position of the average man, who cannot for the life of him see the use of leaving all that is pleasant and dear, of fighting, marching, sickening, and dying for the sake of a cause he does not understand or believe in, as the slave of men whom he perhaps despises. Joseph Berta, the lame conscript, the shrewd, kindly Jew Mathieu, the common-sense miller Christian Weber, protagonists in three well-known stories, each distinct from the other, are all alike in their preference for peace over war, for the joy of home and the quiet prosecution of their respective affairs, instead of the dubious pleasures of siege and campaign.

There is a superbly *bourgeois* flavour to it all. Yet one feels its force, its sound humanity. The republicanism of these writers is of the broadest kind. They hate Bonaparte or Bourbon, because in their belief either house stands for tyranny and corruption ; while Napoleon is their special detestation, the later Empire is vigorously assailed because it, too, is opposed to the interests of the people. Napoleon III., whom in high satiric scorn they pillory as "The Honest Man," comes in for savage condemnation, since he again brings woe upon the working folk, in pursuit of his own selfish ends. And underneath all, like a groundswell can be felt a deep and genuine, if homely, patriotism.

Human nature, as it is witnessed in the pages of Erckmann-Chatrian, is not hard to decipher. It lacks the subtlety of the modern psychologue, miscalled a novelist. Humanity for them is made up of two great contrasted elements—the people and the enemies of the people ; the latter made up of kings, politicians, government leaders, and the general world of bureaucracy, who fleece the former, "that vast flock which they were always accustomed to shear, and which they call the people." But the people themselves, how veritable and charming they are ! Not a whit are they idealized ; the fictional folk of these writers are always recognisable ; they give us that pleasure of recognition which Mr. James points out as one of the principal virtues of modern novel-making. The title of one of the well-known books, *The History of a Man of the People*, might almost stand as a description of their complete works. There is no sentimentalizing of average humanity ; none of the Auerbach or George Sand prettification of country life. Erckmann-Chatrian are as truthful as a later realist like Thomas Hardy. The family life in *The Brigadier Frederick* is almost lyrically set forth, until it seems, mayhap, too good for human nature's daily food; but similar scenes in other stories have a Dutch-like fidelity in their transcripts of the coarser, less lovely human traits; recall the wife and daughter of Weber, for example, or the well-nigh craven fear of Joseph Berta in *The Plebiscite*, who seems half a poltroon until he is seasoned in a Napoleonic campaign; the psychologic treatment here suggesting Stephen Crane's *The Red Badge of Courage*. The blend of grim realism and heroic patriotism in the figure of the old sergeant in *The Plebiscite* is a fine illustration of that truth to both the shell and kernel of life which Erckmann-Chatrian maintain throughout their work.

On the whole, then, it is a comfortable, enheartening conception of Man they present. Poor theologians they would make; men are by nature good and kind; only warped by cruel misuse and bad masters, as in war. "Ah, it is a great joy to love and to be loved, the only one joy of life," exclaims the Jew Mathieu in *The Blockade*. This simple yet sufficient creed pervades their thought. Again and again is it declared that whatever the apparent evil, so that the faithful-hearted and devout of the world, like Father Frederick, lose courage for the moment, the fault is with men upon earth, not in heaven. High over all, God reigns. A spirit of kindliness, quiet, unheroic, but deep and tender, enswathes the more serious part of these novels like an atmosphere ; and if the mood shifts to indignation, it is the righteous indignation of the good in the face of that which is wrong and evil. And these better human attributes are most commonly found in the provinces ; the city, as a rule, spells sin. The touch of mother earth brings purity and strength. " La mauvaise race qui trompe," declares the Brigadier Frederick, "n'existe pas au pays; elle est toujours venue d'ailleurs." One smiles at this, but it offends not nor seems absurd. Its very prejudice is lovable.

Perhaps none of the stories make so moving an appeal against war as *The Brigadier Frederick*. Its sadness is the most heartfelt, its realism the most truthful, and hence effective. Nor in any other book of the War Series does the French character shine more clearly in its typical virtues. Family love and faith, *camaraderie*, humble devoutness in religion, and earnest patriotism are constantly made manifest in this fine tale. Instead of conducting their hero through the spectacular scenes of military campaigns, the authors depict only the stay-at-home aspects of war, which because of their lack of strut and epic colour are, as a rule, overlooked, and which yet illustrate far better than the most Zolaesque details the wretched *milieu* and after effects of a great national struggle. Frederick, the old guard of the Alsatian forest domains, loses in turn his post, his son-in-law, wife, and daughter, and at last his native land; and through all his misery remains proudly a Frenchman, who refuses to declare allegiance to the German invaders; and, in being true to his convictions, furnishes a noble example of a man who, by the moral test, rises superior to any fate, his head being

"bloody but unbowed."

Again, sad as the story is, it differs from too much of the tragedy of current literature; it is sad for the sake of a purpose, not for sadness' sake. Alleviation is offered the reader from the beginning, in that he knows that Frederick himself has survived all his woes, since he is telling his tale to a friend in after years. These qualities make the work wholesome and beautiful, sound both for art and life.

Erckmann-Chatrian draw strength from mother-soil. Their stories are laid in Alsace-Lorraine, or at least it is that debatable land whence the characters go only to return for the peaceful denouement, which these authors, in the good old-fashioned style, like to offer their readers. The popularity of such writers brings us back, happily, to that untechnical valuation of literature which insists, first of all, in regarding it as an exposition of human experience. Their books bear translation especially well because there is something in them besides incommunicable flavours of style, though style is not wanting; namely, vital folk, vivid scenes, significant happenings. Theirs is the misleading simplicity of method and manner which hides technique of a rare and admirable kind. Allowing for all exaggeration for altered ideals in fiction, and for the waning of interest in the historical circumstances which they portray, there remain such elements of permanent appeal as to give their books far more than a transient worth.

For more than forty years, Erckmann-Chatrian wrote as one man; their collaboration was, in effect, a chemical union. No example in literature better illustrates the possibility of the merging of individualities for the purposes of artistic unity. The double work of the English Besant and Rice is by no means so important nor do they stand and fall together in the same sense; much of Besant's typical fiction being produced after his partner's death. In the case of the most famed collaboration of older days, that of the dramatists

Erckmann–Chatrian

Beaumont and Fletcher, the union was more intimate. But the early death of Beaumont, the consideration that he wrote less than half the plays conventionally attributed to their joint authorship, and the additional consideration that some of the best and most enjoyable dramas associated with these great names—*The Loyal Subject*, to mention but one—are unquestionably of Fletcher's sole composition, make the Beaumont-Fletcher alliance not so perfect an example of literary collaboration as is offered by Erckmann-Chatrian. When Chatrian died in 1890, it was as if, for literary purposes, both died. Their work had a unity testifying to a remarkable if not unique congeniality in temperament, view and aim, as well as to a fraternal unity which—alas ! the irony of all human friendships—was dispelled when their quarrel, just before the death of Chatrian, put an end to an association so fruitful and famous.

From the very nature of fiction in contrast with drama, it would seem as if collaboration in stage literature were more likely to yield happy results than in the case of the novel. Here, however, is an example setting aside *a priori* reasoning ; seemingly " helpless each without the other," the final breach in their personal relations would seem to have written Finis to their literary endeavour. Yet Erckmann survived for nearly a decade and wrote military stories, which in tone and temper carried on the traditions of the two men. But we may easily detect in this last effort the penalty of their literary severance : the loss of the craftsmanship of Chatrian was a loss indeed. Nor is this subjective guess-work of the critic ; Erckmann himself described nearly twenty years ago the respective parts played by the two in their literary work. He declared that after a story had been blocked out and thoroughly talked over between them, he did all the actual composition. Then was it Chatrian's business to point out faults, to suggest, here a change in perspective, there less emphasis upon a subsidiary character, or here again, a better handling of proportion—in short, to do all the retouching that looks to artistry. And Erckmann goes on to testify in good set terms how necessary his collaborator was to the final perfected form of the story ; how much it must have suffered without his sense of technique. It would appear from this that the senior member of the firm did what is commonly called the creative work of composition, the junior filling the rôle of critic. From France one hears that Erckmann was very German in taste and sympathy (*mirabile dictu !* in view of so much of what he

Erckmann–Chatrian

wrote); Chatrian, French to the core, a man who insisted on residing on the French side of the national line, who reared his sons to be French soldiers; whereas Erckmann in later years hobnobbed with the Germans, members of his family, in fact, intermarrying with his ancient enemies.

Indeed, this last act of their personal history has its disillusionment. But after all, men shall be judged in their works. Whatever their private quarrellings, their respective parts in literary labour, their attributes or national leanings, the world, justly caring most in the long run for the fiction they wrote, will continue to think of them as provincial patriots, lovers of their country, and Frenchmen of the French, not only in the tongue they used, but in those deep-lying characteristics and qualities which make their production worthily Gallic in the nobler implication of the word.

RICHARD BURTON.

BIOGRAPHICAL NOTE

The celebrated friends who collaborated for fifty years under the title of ERCKMANN-CHATRIAN *were natives of the department of the Meurthe, in Alsace-Lorraine.* ÉMILE ERCKMANN *was born at Phalsbourg (now Pfalzburg), on the 20th of May, 1822. His father was a bookseller; his mother he lost early. He was educated at the grammar school of Phalsbourg, and was a boarder there, growing up an intractable and idle boy. At the age of twenty Erckmann went up to Paris to study law, but he was inattentive to his work, and positively took fifteen years to pass the necessary examinations; having done so, he made no further use of his profession. When he was twenty-five he suffered from a serious illness, and during his convalescence, in Alsace, he turned his attention to literature. At this moment there had arrived in Phalsbourg, as an usher in the grammar school, a young Alsatian,* ALEXANDRE CHATRIAN, *of Italian descent, who was born at Soldatenthal, near*

Biographical Note

Abreschwiller, on the 18th of December, 1826, and who was destined for the trade of glass-worker. He had been sent in 1844, as an apprentice, to the glass-works in Belgium, but had, in opposition to the wish of his parents, determined to return and to be a schoolmaster in France.

Erckmann and Chatrian now met, and instantly felt irresistibly drawn to one another. From this time until near the end of their careers their names were melted indissolubly into one. In 1848 a local newspaper, " Le Démocrate du Rhin," opened its columns to their contributions, and they began to publish novels. Their first great success was " L'Illustre Docteur Mathéus," in 1859, which appeared originally in the " Revue Nouvelle," and which exactly gauged the taste of the general public. This was followed by " Contes Fantastiques" and " Contes de la Montagne," in 1860 ; by " Maître Daniel Rock," in 1861 ; by " Contes des Bords du Rhin" and " Le Fou Yégof," in 1862 ; " Le Joueur de Clarinette," in 1863 ; and in 1864, which was perhaps the culminating year of the talent of Erckmann-Chatrian, by " Madame Thérèse," " L'Ami Fritz," and " L'Histoire d'un Conscrit de 1813." These, and innumerable stories which followed them, dealt almost entirely with scenes of country life in Alsace and the neighbouring German Palat-

Biographical Note

inate. The authors adopted a strong Chauvinist bias, and at the time of the Franco-German War their sympathies were violently enlisted on the side of France.

In 1872 Erckmann-Chatrian published a political novel which enjoyed an immense success, " Histoire du Plébiscite "; in 1873, " Les Deux Frères "; and they concluded in many volumes their long romance " Histoire d'un Paysan." Two of the latest of their really striking romances were " Les Vieux de la Vielle," 1882, and " Les Rantzau," 1884. During this period, however, their great vogue was the theatre, where in 1869 they produced " Le Juif Polonais," and in 1877 " L'Ami Fritz," two of the most successful romantic plays of the nineteenth century, destined to be popular in all parts of the world. After the war of 1870–'71 Erckmann lived at Phalsbourg, which was presently annexed to German Lothringen, and he became a German citizen; Chatrian continued to reside in Paris, and remained a Frenchman. For a long time the friends continued to collaborate on the old terms of intimacy, though at a distance from one another, but a quarrel finally separated them, on a vulgar matter of interest. Erckmann claimed, and Chatrian refused, author's rights on those plays which bore the name of both writers,

Biographical Note

although Chatrian had composed them unaided. The rupture became complete in 1889, when the old friends parted as bitter enemies. Chatrian died a year later, on the 4th of September, 1890, from a stroke of apoplexy, at Villemomble, near Paris. Erckmann left Phalsbourg, and settled at Lunéville, where he died on the 14th of March, 1899. The temperament of Erckmann was phlegmatic and melancholy; that of Chatrian impetuous and fiery. They were strongly opposed to the theories of the realists, which assailed them in their advancing age, and they stated their own principles of literary composition in " Quelques mots sur l'esprit humain," 1880, and its continuation " L'Art et les Grands Idéalistes," 1885. For a long time their popularity was unequalled by that of any other French novelist, largely because their lively writings were pre-eminently suited to family reading. But they never achieved an equal prominence in purely literary estimation.

E. G.

CONTENTS

'ey

BRIGADIER FREDERICK

I

WHEN I was brigadier forester at Steinbach, said Father Frederick to me, and when I was the inspector of the most beautiful forest district in all the department of Saverne, I had a pretty cottage, shaded by trees, the garden and orchard behind filled with apple trees, plum trees, and pear trees, covered with fruit in the autumn; with that four acres of meadow land along the bank of the river; when the grandmother, Anne, in spite of her eighty years, still spun behind the stove, and was able to help about the house; when my wife and daughter kept house and superintended the stables and the cultivation of our land, and when weeks, months, and years passed in their tranquility like a single day. If at that time any one had said to me, "See here, Brigadier Frederick, look at this great valley of Alsace, that extends to the banks of the Rhine; its hundreds of villages, surrounded by harvests of all kinds:

tobacco, hops, madder, hemp, flax, wheat, barl[ey]
and oats, over which rushes the wind as over the
sea ; those high factory chimneys, vomiting clouds
of smoke into the air ; those wind-mills and saw-
mills ; those hills, covered with vines ; those great
forests of beech and fir trees, the best in France
for ship-building ; those old castles, in ruins for
centuries past, on the summits of the mountains ;
those fortresses of Neuf-Brisach, Schlestadt, Phalsbourg, Bitche, that defend the passes of the
Vosges. Look, brigadier, as far as a man's eye
can reach from the line of Wissembourg to Belfort. Well, in a few years all that will belong to
the Prussians ; they will be the masters of all ;
they will have garrisons everywhere ; they will
levy taxes ; they will send preceptors, censors,
foresters, and schoolmasters into all the villages,
and the inhabitants will bend their backs ; they
will go through the military drill in the German
ranks, commanded by the *feldwebel** of the Emperor William." If any one had told me that, I
would have thought the man was mad, and, even
in my indignation, I should have been very likely
to have given him a backhander across the face.

He would only have told the truth, however,
and he would not even have said enough, for we

---

* Sergeant.

have seen many other things; and the most terrible thing of all for me, who had never quitted
the mountain, is to see myself, at my old age, in
this garret, from which I can see only the tiles
and chimney-pots; alone, abandoned by Heaven
and earth, and thinking day and night of that
frightful story.

Yes, George, the most terrible thing is to
think! Foxes and wolves that are wounded lick
themselves and get well. Kids and hares that are
hurt either die at once, or else hide in a thicket
and end by recovering. When a dog's puppies
are taken away, the poor beast pines for a few
days; then she forgets, and all is forgotten. But
we men cannot forget, and as time goes on we
realize our misery more and more, and we see
many sad things that we had not felt at first. Injustice, bad faith, selfishness, all grow up before
our eyes like thorns and briers.

However, since you desire to know how I happened to get into this hovel in the heart of La
Villette, and the way in which I have passed my
life up to the present time, I will not refuse to
answer you. You can question many other people
beside myself; persons of different occupations—
workmen, peasants emigrated from down yonder;
all the tumble-down houses of La Villette and La

Chapelle are filled with them. I have heard that more than two hundred thousand hav left. It is possible. When I quitted the country the roads were already overcrowded.

But you know all about these things as well as I do ; so I will tell about what concerns me alone, beginning at the beginning. That will be the simplest way,

When your grandfather, M. Münsch, the President of the Tribunal, obtained promotion, in 1865, and left for Brittany, I was very glad of it, in one way, for he deserved to be promoted ; I have never seen a better or more learned man. Saverne was not the place for him. But, on the other hand, I was very sorry for it. My father, the former forester of Dôsenheim, had never spoken to me of President Münsch but with the greatest respect, repeating to me, over and over again, that he was our benefactor, that he had always liked our family. I myself owed to him my good post at Steinbach, and it was also on his recommendation that I got my wife, Catherine Burat, the only daughter of the former brigadier, Martin Burat.

After that, you can readily believe that, in going to make my report at Saverne, it was always with emotion that I gazed upon that good house, where, for twenty years, I had been so kindly received, and I regretted that noble man; it made my heart very sad. And, naturally, we missed very much, no longer having you to spend the vacations with us. We were so used to having you, that, long in advance, we would say: "The month of September is coming round; little George will soon be here."

My wife arranged the bed upstairs; she put lavender in the well-bleached sheets, and she washed the floor and window-panes. I prepared snares for the thrushes and bait of all kinds for the trout; I repaired the tomtits' hut under the rocks; I tried the whistles for the bird-calls, and made new ones with lead and geese bones; I arranged everything in order in our boxes—the hooks, the lines, the flies, made of cock feathers; laughing beforehand at the pleasure of seeing you rummage among them, and of hearing you say: "See here, Father Frederick, you must wake me up to-morrow morning at two o'clock, without fail; we will start long before day!"

I knew very well that you would sleep like a top till I should come to shake you and to scold you for your laziness; but at night, before going to bed, you always wanted to be up at two o'clock, or even at midnight; that amused me greatly.

And then I saw you in the hut, keeping so

still while I whistled on the bird-call that you scarcely dared to breathe; I heard you trembling on the moss when the jackdaws and thrushes arrived, wheeling under the trees to see; I heard you whisper, softly: "There they are, there they are!"

You were almost beside yourself when there came a great cloud of tomtits, which usually happened just at daybreak.

Yes, George, all these things rejoiced my heart, and I looked forward to the vacations with as much impatience perhaps as you did. Our little Marie-Rose also rejoiced in the thought of soon seeing you again; she hastened to plait new snares and to repair the meshes of the nets which had got broken the year before. But then all was over; you were never to return, and we knew it well.

Two or three times that poor idiot Calas, who looked after our cows in the field, seeing afar off on the other slope of the valley some persons who were on their way to Dôsenheim, came running in, crying, with his mouth open as far as his ears, "Here he is, here he is! It is he; I recognise him; he has his bundle under his arm!"

And Ragot barked at the heels of that idiot. I should have liked to have knocked them both over, for we had learned of your arrival at Rennes, and the President himself had written that you re-gretted Steinbach every day. I was in a bad enough humour, without listening to such cries.

Often, too, my wife and Marie-Rose, while ar-ranging the fruit on the garret floor, would say : " What fine melting pears, what good gray rennets ! Ah ! if George returned, he would roll them round from morning till night. He would do nothing but run up and down stairs." And then they would smile, with tears in their eyes.

And how often I myself, returning from the bird-catching, and throwing on the table my bunches of tomtits, have I not cried : " Look ! there are ten or twelve dozen of them. What is the good of them now the boy is no longer here ? Might as well give them to the cat ; for my part, I despise them."

That was true, George ; I never had a taste for tomtits, or even for thrushes. I always liked bet-ter a good quarter of beef, with now and then only a little bit of game, by way of change.

Well, it is thus that the time passed just after your departure. That lasted for some months, and finally our ideas took another course, and that the more because, in the month of January, 1867, a great misfortune happened to us.

Brigadier Frederick

II

In the depth of the winter, while all the roads and the mountain paths were covered with snow, and we heard every night the branches of the beech trees breaking like glass under their load of ice, to the right and left of the house, one evening my wife, who, since the commencement of the season, had gone to and fro looking very pale and without speaking, said to me, towards six o'clock, after having lighted the fire in the fireplace, "Frederick, I am going to bed. I do not feel well. I am cold."

She had never said anything like that before. She was a woman who never complained and who, during her youth, had looked after her house up to the very day before her confinements. I suspected nothing, and I replied to her :

"Catherine, do not put yourself out. You work too hard. Go and rest. Marie Rose will do the cooking."

I thought "once in twenty years is not too much ; she may well rest herself a little."

Marie-Rose heated a jug of water to put under her feet, and we took our supper of potatoes and clotted milk as tranquilly as usual. We were not at all uneasy, and about nine o'clock, having smoked my pipe near the stove, I was about to go to bed, when, on coming near the bed, I saw my wife, white as a sheet, and with her eyes wide open. I said to her,

"Helloa, Catherine!"

But she did not stir. I repeated "Catherine," and shook her by the arm. She was already cold.

The courageous woman had not lain down till the last moment, so to speak; she had lost much blood without complaining. I was a widower. My poor Marie-Rose no longer had a mother.

That crushed me terribly. I thought I should never recover from the blow.

The old grandmother, who for some time had scarcely ever stirred from her arm-chair, and who seemed always in a dream, awoke. Marie-Rose uttered cries and sobs which could be heard out of doors, and even Calas, the poor idiot, stammered:

"Oh, if I had only died instead of her!"

And as we were far away in the woods, I was forced to transport my poor wife to bury her, to the church at Dôsenheim, through the great snows. We went in a line, with the coffin before us in the cart. Marie-Rose·wept so much that I was forced to support her at every step. Fortunately the grandmother did not come; she sat at home in her arm-chair, reciting the prayers for the dead.

Brigadier Frederick

We did not return that evening till it was dark night. And now the mother was yonder under the snow, with the old Burat family, who are all in the cemetery of Dôsenheim behind the church; she was there, and I thought:

"What will become of the house? Frederick, you will never marry again; you have had a good wife and who knows if the second would not be the worst and the most extravagant in the country. You will never take another. You will live like that, all alone. But what will you do? Who will take care of everything? Who will look after your interest day and night? The grandmother is too old and the girl is still a mere child."

I was miserable, thinking that everything would go to ruin and that my savings of so many years would be wasted from day to day.

But my little Marie-Rose was a real treasure, a girl full of courage and good sense, and no sooner was my wife dead than she put herself at the head of our affairs, looking after the fields, the cattle, and the household, and ruling Calas like her mother. The poor fellow obeyed her; he understood in his simplicity that she was now the mistress and that she had the right to speak for everybody.

And so things go on earth. When we have

had such trials we think that nothing worse can happen to us, but all that was merely the beginning, and when I think of it, it seems to me that our greatest happiness would have been, all to have died together upon the same day.

III

THUS all our joys, all our satisfactions passed away, one after the other. The old house to which I formerly returned, laughing from afar, only to see its little windows glittering in the sun and its little chimney smoking between the tops of the fir trees, was then sad and desolate. The winter appeared very long to us. The fire which sparkles so joyously on the hearth when the white flowers of the frost cover the panes, and when silence reigns in the valley, that fire which I had so often gazed at for half an hour at a time while smoking my pipe, thinking of a thousand things that passed through my head, now gave me none but melancholy thoughts. The fagots wept; poor Ragot sought in every corner, he wandered up stairs and down and smelt under all the doors; Caïas wove baskets in silence, the oziers piled in front of him; grandmother Anne told her beads, and Marie-Rose, very pale and dressed in black, came and went through the house, watching over all and doing everything without noise like her poor mother. As for me, I said nothing; when death has entered anywhere all lamentations that one makes are pure loss. Yes, that winter was long!

And then the spring came as in other years; the firs and beech trees put forth their buds; the windows were opened to renew the air : the great pear tree before the door became covered with white flowers; all the birds of the air began once more to sing, to chase each other, and to build nests as if nothing had happened.

I also returned to my work, accompanying the chief guard, M. Rameau, in his circuits in order to direct the wood felling, overlooking the works from a distance, leaving early in the morning and returning late, at the last song of the thrushes.

My grief pursued me everywhere, and yet I had still the consolation of seeing Marie-Rose grow in strength and beauty in a truly marvellous way.

It is not, George, because I was her father that I tell you this, but you would have had to search for a long time from Saverne to Lutzelstein before finding as fresh-looking a young girl with as trim a figure, as honest an air, with such beautiful blue eyes and such magnificent fair hair. And how well she understood all kinds of work, whether in the house or out of doors! Ah, yes, I may well say it, she was a beautiful creature, gentle and yet strong.

Often coming in at night and seeing her at the head of the stairs, signing to me that she had waited supper a long time for me, then running down the stairs and holding out to me her fresh cheek, I have often thought:

" She is still handsomer than her mother was at the same age ; she has the same good sense. Don't lament over your misfortunes, Frederick, for many people would envy your lot in having such a child, who gives you so much satisfaction."

One thing only made the tears come, that is when I thought of my wife, then I cried to myself :

"Ah ! if Catherine could come back to see her, she would be very happy !"

About the same time other ideas entered my head ; the epoch of my retirement was approaching, and as Marie-Rose had entered her seventeenth year, I thought of finding her a good and nice young fellow from among the foresters, in whose house I could tranquilly end my days, in the midst of my children and grandchildren, and who, taking my place, would respect me as I had respected my father-in-law Burat, when succeeding him twenty years before.

I thought of it ; it was my principal idea, and I had even some one in view, a tall and handsome young man from Felsberg, who had left the horse guards three or four years before, and who had just been appointed forest guard at Tömenthal, near our house. His name was Jean Merlin, and he was already experienced in the duties of a forester, having passed his apprenticeship at Eyisheim, in Alsace.

The young fellow pleased me first because he had a good character, afterward because Marie-Rose regarded him with a favourable eye. I had remarked that she always blushed a little when she saw him enter the house to make his report, and that he never failed to appear in full dress, carefully shaved, his little cap with its hunting horn badge, adorned with an oak leaf or a sprig of heather, which sets off a man ; and that his voice, which was a little gruff, became very gentle in saying, "Good day, Mlle. Marie-Rose ; I hope you are quite well ? What beautiful weather we are having—the sun is shining finely," etc. He appeared embarrassed ; and Marie-Rose also answered him timidly. It was very clear that they loved and admired each other, a natural thing when one is old enough to get married. It always has been and always will be so ; it is a blessing of Providence.

Therefore I found no evil in it, on the contrary I thought : "When he asks her of me according to custom, we will see about it. I will say neither yes nor no at once ; one must not have the air of throwing one's self at people's heads ; but I will, and by yielding, for neither must one break young people's hearts."

Those were the ideas that I revolved in my head.

Besides which the young man was of good family ; he had his uncle, Daniel Merlin, who was schoolmaster at Felsberg ; his father had been sergeant in a regiment of infantry, and his mother, Margredel, though she lived with him in the forester's house at Tömenthal, possessed at Felsberg a cottage, a garden, and four or five acres of good land ; one could not desire a match in every way more advantageous.

And seeing that everything seemed to go according to my wishes, almost every evening when I returned from my circuits through the woods, in the path which skirts the valley of Dôsenheim, at the moment when the sun is setting, when the silence spreads itself with the shadow of the forest

over the great meadows of La Zinzelle—that silence of the solitude, scarcely broken by the murmur of the little river—almost every evening,
walking thoughtfully along, I pictured to myself
the peace that my children would have in this
corner of the world, their pleasant home, the birth
of little beings whom we would carry to Dôsenheim to have them baptized in the old church,
and other similar things, which touched my heart
and made me say :

"Lord God, it is all sure ; these things will
happen. And when you grow old, Frederick,
very old, your back bent by age, like grandmother
Anne, and your head quite white, you will pass
away quietly, satisfied with years, and blessing the
young brood. And long after you are gone, that
brave Jean Merlin, with Marie-Rose, will keep
you in remembrance."

In picturing all this to myself, I halted regularly on the path above the forester house of Jean
Merlin, looking beneath at the little tiled roof,
the garden surrounded with palisades, and the
yard whence the mother of Jean drove her ducks
and fowls into the poultry-yard towards night, for
foxes were not wanting in that outskirt of the forest. I looked down from above, and I cried, raising my cap, " Hilloa ! Margredel, good evening."

Brigadier Frederick

Then she would raise her eyes, and joyously reply to me, "Good evening, Mr. Brigadier. Are all well at your house?"

"Why, yes, Margredel, very well, Heaven be praised." Then I would come down through the brushwood, and we would shake hands.

She was a good woman, always gay and laughing, because of her great confidence in God, which made her always look upon the bright side of things. Without ever having said anything to each other, we knew very well of what we were each thinking; we only needed to talk about the weather to understand all the rest.

And when, after having had a good gossip, I went away, Margredel would still call after me, in her rather cracked voice, for she was nearly sixty years old, "A pleasant walk to you, Brigadier. Don't forget Mlle. Marie-Rose and the grandmother."

"Don't be afraid. I'll forget nothing."

She would make a sign with her head to me that it was all right, and I would go off with lengthening steps.

It sometimes happened to me also, sometimes when my circuit was finished before five o'clock, to find Jean near the house, at the other side of the valley, in the path that skirted our orchard, and Marie-Rose in the garden picking vegetables. They were each on their own side, and were talking across the hedge without appearing to do so ; they were telling things to each other.

That reminded me of the happy time when I was courting Catherine, and I came up very softly over the heather till I was within twenty steps behind them, and then I cried, " Ho ! ho ! Jean Merlin, is it like this that you perform your duties ? I catch you saying fine words to the pretty girls."

Then he turned round, and I saw his embarrassed look.

" Excuse me, Brigadier," he said, " I came to see you on business, and I was conversing with Mlle. Marie-Rose while waiting.for you."

" Oh, yes, that is all very well ; we will see to that. I do not trust foxes myself."

And other jokes without end. You can understand, George, that happiness had returned to us.

I had as much confidence in Jean Merlin as in Marie-Rose and in myself. The evil race that deceives does not exist in our country ; it has always come from elsewhere.

Brigadier Frederick

IV

THINGS went on like this throughout the whole year 1868. Jean Merlin took every possible occasion to present himself at the house, either on business connected with his office, or else to consult me on his family affairs. He had but one fear, that was of being refused. Sometimes, when we were walking together in the woods, I saw him musing, with drooping head; he seemed to wish to speak; he raised his voice suddenly, and then was silent.

For my part, I wished that he would be a little more courageous, but I could not open the subject; that would not have been proper for his superior; I awaited his formal proposal, thinking that he would end by writing to me, or by sending me one of his relatives to make a ceremonious declaration: his uncle Daniel, for instance, the schoolmaster of Felsberg, a respectable man, who was able to take charge of so delicate a commission.

It often happened to me also to reflect upon what concerned me particularly. I asked nothing better than to see my daughter happy, but I had to try to arrange all interests in accord as much as possible. When one thinks of nothing, everything appears simple and easy, and yet the best things have their evil side.

I had still nearly two years to serve before retiring, but after that, if my son-in-law was not named brigadier in my place, we would be forced to quit the old house, where I had passed so many years, with the beings who were dear to me—father-in-law Burat, my poor wife, grandmother Anne, everybody, in fact; and we would be obliged to abandon all that to go live in a land which I did not know, and among strange faces.

That idea made me wretched. I knew well that Marie-Rose and Jean Merlin would always respect me as their father; of that I was sure. But the habit of turning round in the same corner and of seeing the same things becomes a second nature, and that is why old hares and old foxes, even when they have received gunshot wounds in the neighbourhood of their lair or their hole, always return there; they need the sight of the brushwood and the tuft of grass, which recall to them their youth, their love, and even the annoyances and the sorrows which, in the long run, make up three-quarters of our existence, and to which we become as strongly attached as to memories of happiness.

Ah! I never should have believed that anything worse could happen to me than to retire with my children into a country of fir trees like ours, and into a little house like my own.

These things made me very uneasy, and, since the departure of President Münsch, I no longer knew of whom I could ask a bit of good advice, when at length all was settled in a very happy way, which touches my heart even now when I think of it.

V

You must know that, during the years 1867, 1868, and 1869, roads were being made in all directions, to facilitate the wood-cutting and to transport the wood to the railway and the canal. M. Laroche, Forest Inspector of the Canton of Lutzelstein, directed these great works. He was a man of fifty-five years of age, robust and serious, who thought of nothing but his business ; hunting and fishing were not among his tastes ; to be well noticed by him, there was no question of being a good shot or a skilful trapper ; it was necessary to serve him well.

He often came himself to the place, explaining clearly the declivity to be followed, the trees which ought to be felled, etc. ; unless one was idiotic, he could not but understand. Things went on this way briskly and well. Naturally, such a man would know all his workmen thoroughly, and when he was satisfied, he would address to you some of those kind words that make your heart light.

For my part, I think that he took an interest in me, for often, after hearing my report in his office at Lutzelstein, he would say to me, "That is very good, very good, Father Frederick!" and would even shake hands with me.

Towards the spring of 1869 the order arrived to repair the road which descends from Petite Pierre to the valley of Graufthal, in order to join the new highway from Saverne to Metting; the junction fell near the saw-mill, not far from the forester's house; I had to go, therefore, every working day with my brigade to survey the works.

The first part was almost finished, and they had commenced to blow up the rocks below, near the valley, to level the road, when, one morning, going to make my usual report at Lutzelstein, the inspector received me particularly well.

It was about ten o'clock, his breakfast hour, and he had just reached his house as I rang.

"Ah! it is you, Father Frederick," said he,

gaily, as he opened his door; "fine weather this morning. All right down yonder?"

"Yes, sir, all is going well, according to your orders."

"Very good," said he. "Sit down, I have something to say to you. You will breakfast with me. My wife is with her parents in Champagne; you will keep me company."

Often, when I arrived at breakfast time, he would offer me a glass of wine, but the idea had never occurred to him to give me a place at his table.

"Sit down there," said he. "Here, Virginie, bring a plate for the brigadier. You can bring in breakfast."

Imagine my astonishment and my satisfaction. I did not know how to thank him; he did not seem to see my embarrassment. He commenced by taking off his tunic and putting on his coat, asking me: "You have a good appetite, Father Frederick?"

"Yes, sir, that never fails me."

"So much the better! Taste this beefsteak; Virginie is a good cook; you will tell me what you think of it. Here's to your health!"

"Here's to yours, sir."

I felt as if I were dreaming; I said to myself,

Brigadier Frederick

" Is this really you, Frederick, who are breakfasting here in this handsome room, with your superior, and who are drinking this good wine?" And I felt embarrassed.

M. Laroche, on the contrary, grew more and more familiar, so that, finally, after three or four glasses, I discovered that the thing was quite natural. Because his wife was not at home, I thought that he was glad to have me to talk over the felling of the timber, the new clearings, and our road from Graufthal; so I grew bolder, and answered him laughing, and almost without embarrassment.

Things went on thus for about twenty minutes; Mlle. Virginie had brought in the biscuits, almonds, and Gruyère cheese, when, throwing himself back in his chair, and looking at me good-humouredly, " It is very agreeable," said he, " to be as well as we are, at our age. Ha! ha! ha! we have not yet lost our teeth, Father Frederick!"

" No, indeed; they are well-rooted, sir." And I laughed, too.

" How old are you?" he asked.

" I shall soon be fifty, sir."

" And I am fifty-five. Well, well, it is all the same; the time for retiring is approaching; one of these days they will slit our ears."

Brigadier Frederick

He was still laughing. As for me, when I thought of that, I was not so gay as before.

Then he passed me the cheese, saying : "What do you think of doing two years from now? For my part, my wife wants to take me into her country, Champagne. That is a great bore; I do not like the plains; but, you know, 'A wilful woman will have her way.' It is a proverb, and all proverbs have an astounding air of good sense."

"Yes, sir," I answered; "such proverbs as that are really annoying, for I could never leave the mountains; I am too used to them. If I had to go, I should not live two weeks. There would be nothing left to do but throw on me the last handful of earth."

"Without doubt," he said; "but when the young people come, the old people must give up their place."

In spite of the good wine, I had become quite silent, thinking of those unfortunate things, when he said to me : "In your place, Father Frederick, do you know what I would do? Since you love the mountains so, since it is, so to speak, your existence to live in the forest—well, I would look out for a son-in-law among the foresters; a good fellow, who would take my place and with whom

I would live tranquilly till the end, in the midst of the green caps and the smell of the firs."

"Ah! that is so, sir; I think of it every day; but——"

"But what?" he said. "What hinders you? You have a pretty daughter, you are a sensible man; what embarrasses you? It is not for want of choice, I hope; in the inspector's guard, big Kern, Donadieu, Nicolas Trompette, would ask nothing better than to become your son-in-law. And that good Jean Merlin. He is what one might call a model forester—frank, active, intelligent, and who would answer your purpose admirably. His record is excellent; he stands first on the list for promotion, and, upon my word, Father Frederick, I think that, on your retreat, he has a good chance of succeeding you."

When I heard that, I got red up to my ears, and I could not help saying, "That is true! No one has anything to say against Jean Merlin; I have never seen a better or more honest fellow; but I cannot offer my daughter to people who please me; Merlin has never spoken to me of marriage with Marie-Rose, neither has his mother Margredel, nor his uncle Daniel; not any of the family. You can understand, sir, that I cannot make the advances; it would not be proper! Beside, everything ought to be done decently and in order; the proposal ought to be made regularly!"

He was going to answer, when Mlle. Virginie came in to pour out the coffee, so he took a box from the mantelpiece, saying, "Let us light our cigars, Father Frederick."

I saw that he was amused, and when the servant went out he cried, laughing, "Come, now, Father Frederick, do you really need some one to tell you that Marie-Rose and Jean Merlin love each other with all their hearts? And must Uncle Daniel come and declare it to you in a black hood and with buckled shoes?"

He laughed loudly, and as I sat in surprise:

"Well," said he, "here is the affair in two words: The other day Jean Merlin was so melancholy that I asked him if he was sick, and the poor fellow confessed to me, with tears in his eyes, what he called his misfortune. You are so serious and respectable-looking that none of the family dared to make the proposal, and the good people thought that I would have some influence. Must I put on my grand uniform, Father Frederick?"

He was so gay that, notwithstanding my trouble, I answered: "Oh, sir, now all is well!"

"Then you consent?"

" Do I consent ? I have never wished for anything else. Yes, yes, I consent, and I thank you. You can say, M. Laroche, that to-day you have rendered Frederick the happiest of men."

I had already risen and had put my bag upon my shoulder, when the chief guard, Rameau, entered, on business connected with the service.

"You are going, Frederick?" asked the inspector. "Are you not going to empty your cup?"

"Ah! M. Laroche," I said, "I am too happy to keep quiet. The children are waiting for me, I am sure ; I must go carry them the good news."

"Go, then, go," he said, rising and accompanying me to the door; "you are right not to delay the young people's happiness."

He shook hands with me, and I left, after saluting M. Rameau.

VI

I went away so happy that I could not see clearly. It was only at the end of the street, in going down at the left again, towards the valley, that I awoke from this great confusion of joyous ideas.

Brigadier Frederick

I had perhaps taken a little drop too much; I must confess, George, that the good wine had dazzled my eyes a little; but my legs were solid, nevertheless, and I went as if I were just twenty years old, laughing and saying to myself:

"Frederick, now everything is according to rule, no one will have anything to say; it is the inspector himself who has made the proposal and that is a thousand times better than if it had been Uncle Daniel. Ha! ha! ha! what luck! Won't they be happy when they learn that I consent; that all is arranged and that there is nothing left to do but to sing the *Gloria in Excelsis*? Ha! ha! ha! And you can laugh, too, for all has gone as you wished it. You will stay in this country to the end of your existence; you will see the woods from your window, and you will smell the sweet odours of the resin and the moss till you are eighty years of age. That is what you needed, to say nothing of the rest; of the children, the grand-children, etc."

I wanted to dance as I descended the Fromuhle road.

It was then about six o'clock, and night was approaching; with the coolness of the evening the frogs were beginning their music in the midst of the reeds, and the high grasses of the pool, and

31

the old fir trees on the other side of the shore showed blue against the darker sky. I stopped from time to time to look at them and I thought:

"You are fine trees, straight and full of good sap, and so you will remain there for a long time to come. The sun will delight your evergreen tops till you are marked for the axe of the wood-cutter. Then that will be the end, but the little firs will have grown up in your shadow and the place will never be vacant."

And while thinking of that, I recommenced my march, quite touched, and I cried:

"Yes, Frederick, such will be your lot. You loved father-in-law Burat, you supported him when he could not do anything, in consideration of the confidence he had reposed in you, and because he was a good man, an old servant of the state and a man to be respected. Now it is your turn to be loved and supported by those who are full of youth; you will be in the midst of them like one of these old fir trees, covered with white moss. The poor old things, they deserved to live, for if they had not grown up straight they would have been cut down long ago to be made into logs and fagots."

I blessed Providence which never lets the honest perish, and it is thus that I arrived, towards seven o'clock in the evening, on the Scienie road at the bottom of the valley. I saw the forester house at the left, near the bridge. Ragot was barking, Calas was bringing the cattle back to the stable, shouting and cracking his whip, the flock of ducks on the bank of the river were scratching and picking themselves around their necks and under their wings and tails, while awaiting the hour of going to roost; some chickens were still pecking in the courtyard, and two or three half-plucked old hens were napping in the shadow of the little wall.

Then, seeing Ragot running to meet me, I said to myself :

" Here we are. Now attention. First you are going to speak. Jean Merlin must be there for certain. All must be quite clear beforehand."

VII

I WENT up the stairs and I saw Marie-Rose in the lower room, with bare arms ; she was kneading dough and rolling it out flat, with the rolling-pin, on our large table, to make noodles. She had seen me in the distance and continued her work without raising her eyes.

"You are working hard, Marie-Rose," I remarked to her.

"Ah! it is you, father," said she; "I am making noodles."

"Yes, it is I," I replied, hanging my bag against the wall; "I have come from the inspector's. Has any one been here?"

"Yes, father, Jean Merlin came to make his report, but he went away again."

"Ah! he went away again, did he? Very good! he has not gone far, I guess; we have some very important business to talk over!"

I came and went, looking at the dough, the basket of eggs, the little bowl of flour and Marie-Rose, working away without opening her lips.

Finally I stopped and said to her:

"See here, Marie-Rose, it is right to be industrious, but we have something else to do just now. What is this that I have just heard at the inspector's? Is it true that you love Jean Merlin?"

As I spoke she let fall the rolling pin and flushed scarlet.

"Yes," I said; "that's the point! I don't mean to scold you about it; Jean Merlin is a nice fellow, and a good forester, and I am not angry at him. In my time I loved your mother dearly, and father Burat, who was my superior, neither chased me away nor swore at me because of it. It is a natural thing when one is young to think of getting married. But when one wishes to marry an honest girl, one must first ask her of her father, so that every one may be agreed. Everything ought to be conducted sensibly."

She was very much embarrassed, for on hearing that she ran to get a pot of mignonette and placed it on the sill of the open window, an action which filled me with surprise, for my wife, Catherine, had done the same thing on the day of my proposal to call me in ; and almost at once Merlin came out of the clump of trees under the rocks opposite, where I also had hidden, and ran across the meadow as I myself had run, twenty-three years before !

Then, seeing these things, I did also what old Burat had done. I placed myself in the hall before the door of the room, my daughter behind me ; and as Merlin entered, all out of breath, I drew myself up and said to him :

" Merlin, is it true what the inspector tells me ; that you love my daughter and ask her in marriage ? "

" Yes, brigadier," he answered me, placing his hand on his heart, " I love her better than life ! "

At the same time he wished to speak to Marie-Rose, but I cried :

"Stop a minute! You love her and she has found out that she loves you. That is very nice —it is agreeable to love each other! But you must think also of the others, of the old people. When I married Catherine Burat I promised to keep her father and mother till the end of their days, and I have kept my word; like every man of honour; I have loved them, cared for them, and venerated them; they have always had the first place at table, the first glass of wine, the best bed in the house. Grandmother Anne, who still lives, is there to say it. It was only my duty, and if I had not done it I would have been a villain; but they have never had any complaints to make, and on his death-bed father Burat blessed me and said : 'Frederick has always been to us like the best of sons!' I deserve, therefore, to have the same, and I wish to have it because it is just! Well, now that you have heard me, will you promise to be to me what I was to father Burat?"

"Ah! brigadier," said he, "I would be the happiest of men to have you for a father! Yes, yes, I promise to be a good son to you; I promise to love you always and to respect you as you deserve."

Then I was touched, and I said:

"In that case, all right; I give you the hand of Marie-Rose, and you may kiss her."

They kissed each other right before me, like two good children that they were. Marie-Rose wept profusely. I called the grandmother into the little side-room; she came leaning on my arm and blessed us all, saying:

"Now I can die in peace, I have seen my grand-daughter happy, and loved by an honest man."

And all that day till evening she did not stop praying, commending her grand-children to God. Merlin and Marie-Rose did not weary of talking together and looking at each other. I walked to and fro in the large room and told them:

"Now you are affianced. Jean can come whenever he likes, whether I am at home or gone out. The inspector told me that he was first on the list for promotion, and that he would doubtless replace me at my retreat; that cannot be far off now; then we will celebrate the marriage."

This good news augmented their satisfaction.

Night came on, and Jean Merlin, so as not to worry his mother, rose and kissed once more his promised bride. We accompanied him out as far as the great pear tree. The weather was magnificent, the sky glittering with stars; not a bird nor a leaf was stirring, all were sleeping in the valley. And as Merlin pressed my hand I said to him again :

"You will tell your mother, Margredel, to come without fail to-morrow before noon ; Marie-Rose will get you up a good dinner, and we will celebrate the betrothal together; it is the greatest festival in one's life ; and if Uncle Daniel could also come we should be very glad of it."

"Very well, Father Frederick," he said, and then he walked swiftly away.

We went in again with tears in our eyes. And thinking of my poor Catherine, I said to myself:

"There are still some pleasant days in life ; why is my good, my excellent wife no longer with us ?"

It was the only bitter moment I had during that day.

VIII

You understand, George, that after this, all went on well. I had nothing more to think of but my service. Jean Merlin and his mother Margredel came to pass every Sunday at our house.

Brigadier Frederick

It was autumn, the opening of the season for hunting and fishing; the time for bird catching and snare setting in the woods, and for fishing baskets and nets at the river.

The old watchmaker, Baure, of Phalsbourg, arrived, as usual, with his great fishing rod and his bag for the trout; Lafleche, Vignerol, and others, with their bird calls and limed twigs; the gentlemen from Saverne with their dogs and their guns; they whistled, they yelled; they shot hares and sometimes a deer; then all these people came to take lunch and refresh themselves at the forester's house; the smell of frying and of good omelettes, with ham, reached to the garden, and we turned a penny or two at the house that way.

As you know all these things, I have no need to tell you about them.

But this year we saw also arrive quantities of wood-cutters from the Palatinate, from Bavaria, and further; great strapping fellows, with knapsacks on their backs and gaiters with bone buttons on their legs, who were going to Neiderviller, to Laneville, and to Toul to work at wood felling. They passed in bands, their vests hanging from the handles of their axes over their shoulders.

These people emptied their mugs of wine as they passed; they were jolly fellows, who filled

39

the room with smoke from their big porcelain pipes, asking questions about everything, laughing and joking like people who have no trouble about earning their living.

Naturally I was glad to have them stop at our house ; that made business brisk.

I remember at this time a thing which shows the blindness of slow-witted people who are ignorant of what is going on at twenty leagues from home, and who trust to the government without thinking of anything ; a thing of which I am ashamed, for we went so far as to laugh at sensible men, who warned us to be on our guard !

One day our whole house was filled with people from the city and the environs ; some of these strangers among the rest. They were laughing and drinking, and one of the tall Bavarians, with red whiskers and big mustaches, who was before the window, cried :

"What a lovely country ! What magnificent fir trees ! What are those old ruins up there—and this little wood yonder—and that path to the right—and that pass to the left, between the rocks ? Ah ! I have never seen such a country for fruit trees or fine water courses. It is rich ; it is green. Is there not a steeple behind that little wood ? What is the name of that pretty village ? '

Brigadier Frederick

I, who was glad to hear this man so enthusiastic over our valley, I told him about everything in detail.

Baure, Dürr, Vignerol were talking together; they were smoking and going occasionally to the kitchen to see if the omelette was nearly ready, without troubling their heads about anything else.

But near the clock sat Captain Rondeau, who had returned home several months before having retired on a pension, a tall, dry-looking man, with hollow cheeks, wearing his black overcoat buttoned up to the chin, suffering from wounds received in Italy, Africa, and the Crimea, listening without saying anything and drinking a cup of milk because Doctor Semperlin had forbidden him to take anything else.

This went on for a whole hour, when the Bavarians, having emptied their mugs, continued their journey. I followed them to the door to show them the road to Biegelberg; the tall, red-haired man laughed, showing his teeth with a joyous air; finally he shook hands with me and cried, "Thanks," as he went to join his band.

While they were taking their leave, Captain Rondeau, leaning on his cane, was standing in the doorway, and he watched them go off with glittering eyes and compressed lips.

"Who are those people, Father Frederick?"
he said to me. "Do you know them?"

"Those are Germans, captain," I answered
him; "wood-cutters; I do not know any more
about them, except that they are going to Toul,
to work for some contractors there."

"Why do they not employ Frenchmen, these
contractors?"

"Ah! because these wood-cutters are cheaper
than ours; they work for half-price."

The captain frowned, and all at once he said:

"Those are spies; people that came to examine the mountain."

"Spies? How is that?" I answered, in astonishment. "What have they to spy out here?
Have they any reason to meddle in our affairs?"

"They are Prussian spies," he said, dryly;
"they came to take a look at our positions."

Then I believed almost that he was joking
with me, and I said to him:

"But, Captain Rondeau, all the strong points
are set down, and any one can buy maps of the
country at Strasburg, or Nancy, or anywhere."

But, looking at me askance, he exclaimed:

"Maps! maps! And do your maps tell how
much hay, and straw, and wheat, and oats, and
wine, and oxen, and horses and wagons can be put

into requisition in each village for an army on the march? Do they tell you where the mayor lives, or the *curé*, or the postmaster, or the receiver of contributions, so that one can lay one's hand upon them at any minute, or where stables can be found to lodge the horses, and a thousand other things that are useful to know beforehand? Maps, in-deed! Do your maps tell the depth of the streams, or the situation of the fords? Do they point out to you the guides that are best to take or the people that must be seized because they might rouse up the populace?"

And as I remained, my arms hanging at my sides, surprised at these things, of which I had never thought, Father Baure cried from the room:

"Well, captain, who is it that would want to attack us? The Germans? Ha! ha! ha! Let them come! let them come! We'll give them a warm reception. Poor devils! I would not like to be in their skins. Ha! ha! ha! We would settle them! Not one should go out alive from these mountains."

All the others laughed and cried out: "Yes! yes! let them come! Let them try it! We'll give them a good reception!"

Then the captain re-entered the room, and,

looking at big Fischer, who was shouting the loud-
est, he asked of him :

" You would receive them ? With what ? Do
you know what you are talking about ? Where
are our troops, our supplies, our arms ; where,
where, where, I ask of you ? And do you know
how many of them there are, these Germans ? Do
you know that they are a million of men, exer-
cised, disciplined, organized, ready to start at two
weeks' notice—artillery, cavalry, infantry ? Do
you know that ? *You* will receive them !"

" Yes," cried Father Baure, " Phalsbourg, with
Bitche, Lichtenberg, and Schlestadt, would stop
them for twenty years."

Captain Rondeau did not even take the trouble
to reply, and, pointing from the window to the
wood-cutters that were going away, he said to me :

" Look, Father Frederick, look ! Are those
men wood-cutters ? Do our wood-cutters march in
ranks ? do they keep step ? do they keep their
shoulders thrown back and their heads straight,
and do they obey a chief who keeps them in order ?
Do not our wood-cutters and those of the mountains all have rounded shoulders and a heavy gait ?
These men are not even mountaineers ; they come
from the plains; they are spies. Yes, they are
spies, and I mean to have them arrested."

And, without listening to what might be answered, he threw some *sous* on the table in payment for his cup of milk, and went out abruptly.

He was scarcely outside the door when all who were present burst out laughing. I signed to them to be quiet, for that the captain could still hear them; then they held their sides and snuffled through their noses, saying:

"What fun! what fun! The Germans coming to attack us!"

Father Baure, while wiping his eyes with his handkerchief, said:

" He is a good fellow; but he got a rap at the Malakoff, and since then his clock has been out of order, and it always strikes noon at fourteen o'clock."

The others recommenced laughing, like real madmen, so that I thought, George, myself, that the captain had not common sense.

All that comes back to me as if it had taken place yesterday, and two or three days later, having learned that the captain had caused the woodcutters to be arrested in a body at the Lutzelbourg station, and that, their papers being all right, they had obtained authorization to continue their journey into Lorraine, notwithstanding all the representations and the observations of M. Rondeau, I believed decidedly that the worthy man was cracked.

Every time that Baure came to the forester's house he would begin upon the chapter of the German spies, and made me very merry over it. But to-day we have ceased laughing, and I am sure that the jokers of Phalsbourg no longer rub their hands when the *feldwebel* makes his rod whistle while calling to the conscripts on the parade ground, " *Gewehr auf!—Gewehr ab!* " I am sure that this sight has more than once recalled to them the captain's warning.

IX

THIS took place at the end of the autumn of 1869; the valley was already filled with mist; then came the winter: the snow began to whirl before the panes, the fire to crackle in the furnace, and the spinning-wheel of Marie-Rose to hum from morning till night, to the accompaniment of the monotonous ticking of the old clock.

I paced to and fro, smoking my pipe, and thinking of my retreat. Doubtless Marie-Rose thought of it also, and Merlin spoke to me some-times about hurrying up the marriage, which annoyed me considerably, for when I have said my say, I am done, and, since we had agreed to celebrate the marriage the day of his nomination, I did not see the use of talking over an affair already decided.

But the young people were in a hurry; the dulness of the season and the impatience of youth were the causes.

For two months past, Baure, Vignerol, Dürr, and the others came no more; the trees bent under their load of icicles; no one passed the house any more, except some rare travellers afar off in the valley. The history of the captain's spies, which had made me laugh so much, had entirely gone out of my head, when an extraordinary thing proved to me clearly that the old soldier had not been wrong in distrusting the Prussians, and that other people thought of dealing foul blows—people high in rank, in whom we had placed all our confidence.

That year several herds of wild boars ravaged the country. These animals scratched up the newly-sown grain; they dug up the ground in the woods to find roots, and came down every night to tear up the fields around the farms and the hamlets.

The peasants were never done lamenting and complaining; when, finally, we heard that Baron

Brigadier Frederick

Pichard had arrived to organize a general battle. I received at the same time the order to go and join him, at his *rendezvous* of Rothfelz, with the best marksmen of the brigade, as many of the huntsmen of the neighbourhood as I could get.

It was in December I started with Merlin, big Kern, Donadieu, Trompette, and fifteen or twenty hunters, and in the evening we found up there all the baron's guests, filling the rooms of the little hunting lodge, lying on straw, eating, drinking, and joking as usual.

But you know all about those things, George; you remember also the hunting lodge at Rothfelz, the cries of the hunters, the barking of the dogs, and the danger of the guests, who fired in every direction but the right one, in the lines and out of the lines, always imagining at the end that they had killed the great beast. As for us guards, we had always missed. You remember that; it is always the same thing.

What I want to tell you is, that after the hunt, in which some wild boars and a few young pigs had fallen, they had a grand feast in the hunting lodge. The carriages of the baron had contained an abundance of everything : wine, cherry brandy, wheaten bread, pies, sugar, coffee, cognac ; and, naturally, towards midnight, after having run around in the snow, eaten, drunk, howled and sung, the party of pleasure wore a dubious aspect.

We were quartered in the kitchen and well supplied with everything, and, as the door of the dining-room was open, to air the room, we could hear everything that the guests said, particularly as they shouted at the tops of their voices, like blind men.

I had noticed among the number a tall, lean fellow, with a hooked nose, black eyes, a small mustache, a tightly-fitting vest, and muscular legs in his high leather gaiters, who handled his small gun with singular skill; I said to myself, "That man, Frederick, is not in the habit of sitting before a desk and toasting his calves by the fire; he is certainly a soldier, a superior officer!"

He had been stationed near me in the morning, and I had noticed that his two shots had not missed their mark. I looked upon him as a real huntsman, and so he was. He knew also how to drink, for towards midnight three-fourths of the guests were already fast asleep in all the corners, and, except himself, Baron Pichard, M. Tubingue, one of the largest, richest vine-growers in Alsace; M. Jean Claude Ruppert, the notary, who could drink two days running without changing colour or saying one word quicker than another; and M.

Brigadier Frederick

Mouchica, the wood-merchant, whose custom it is to intoxicate every one with whom he has any dealings—except these, the other guests, extended on their bundles of straw, had all left the party.

Then a loud conversation took place; the baron said that the Germans were sending spies into Alsace, that they had agents everywhere, disguised as servants or commercial travellers or peddlers; that they were drawing out maps of the roads, the paths, the forests; that they even penetrated into our arsenals and sent notes regularly to Germany; that they had done the same thing in Schleswig-Holstein before commencing the war, and then in Bohemia, before Sadowa; that they were not to be trusted, etc.

The notary and M. Mouchica agreed with him that it was a very serious business, and that our government ought to take measures to stop this spy system.

Naturally, when we heard that, we listened with all our ears, when the officer began to laugh, saying that he was more ready to believe what the baron said because we were doing the same thing in Germany; that we had engineers in all the fortresses and staff-officers in all their valleys. And M. Tubingue having said that that was impossible, that no French officer would behave that way, because of the honour of the army, he began to laugh still louder, and said :

"But, my dear sir, what is war now? It is an art, a game, an open contest ; they look over each other's hands and each tries to make out the cards of his adversary. Look at me ; I have gone all through the Palatinate as a commercial traveller ; I sold Bordeaux to those good Germans!"

Then, laughing still more, the gentleman related all that he had seen on his road, just like what Captain Rondeau had said that the Prussians were doing here, adding that we were only waiting for an excuse to seize on the left bank of the Rhine.

When they heard that, my guards began to stamp their feet with delight, as if their fortune was made ; and at once the door was closed, and we heard nothing more.

I went out into the air, for the stupidity of big Kern, Trompette, and the others disgusted me.

It was very cold outside ; the platform was white with frost and the moon over the bristling old firs was peeping between the clouds.

"What is the matter, brigadier?" asked Merlin, who had followed me ; "you look pale. Do you feel sick?"

"Yes, the stupidity of Trompette and the

others has upset me ; I should like to know what
made them stamp," I answered. "And you, too,
Merlin ; you surprise me ! You think that it is a
fine thing to invade the country of our neighbours; to carry off the wheat, the wine, the hay,
and the straw of poor people, who never did us
any harm. You think it is fine to take their
country and to make them French, in spite of
themselves. That is sport. You think that is
sport ! Would you like to become a German ?
Would you like to obey the Prussians and put
aside your country for another ? What would it
profit us to do such a thing as that ? Would it
make us richer to tear out the souls of our neighbours ? Would that leave us with a good conscience ? Well, for my part, I would not, for the
honour of our nation, have an ill-gotten *centime*
or inch of land. I do not want to believe what
that gentleman says. If it is true, so much the
worse ! Even if we were the strongest to-day, the
Germans, from father to son, would think only
of vengeance, of returning to their rights, of
reclaiming their blood. Would the good God be
just to abandon them ? There are only beings
without hearts and without religion who are capable of believing it; gamblers, who imagine stu-
pidly that they will always win. Nevertheless, we

see that many gamblers end their days on a dung-
hill."

"Father Frederick," said Merlin, "don't be
angry with me. I had never thought of all that;
it is true. But you are too angry to return to the
kitchen."

"Yes," I answered, "let us go to sleep; that
is better than drinking; there is still room in the
barn."

We did so, and left the next morning at daybreak.

What I have just told you, George, is true; I
have always placed justice above everything, and
even now, when I have lost all that I loved best
in the world, I repeat the same thing. I am better pleased in my great misery to be deprived of
the fruit of my labour for thirty years than to
have lost my love of justice.

———

X

AFTER that the winter passed as usual; rain,
snow, great blasts of wind through the leafless
trees, uprooted firs, dislodged rocks, covering
with earth the roads and paths at the foot of

the slope. That is what I had seen for twenty-five years past.

Then gradually the spring arrived. The cattle again descended to drink at the river. Calas began to sing again as he cracked his whip, and the cock began to flap his wings on the low wall of the poultry-yard, in the midst of his hens, filling with his clear voice all the echoes of the valley.

Ah! how all that comes back to me, George, and how beautiful those things to which I then paid no attention, appear to me now in this garret into which scarcely a ray of light can penetrate.

It was our last spring at the forest house.

Marie-Rose, every morning, in her short petticoat, with her clean *fichu* crossed over her bosom, went into the garden with her basket and the old earthy knife, to gather the first vegetables. She came and went, lifting up the bordering of box that edged the little alleys, and tied up the branches of the rose bushes that had fallen away from their stakes. I saw in the distance Jean Merlin, advancing at a swift pace through the meadow path, skirting the old willows; I heard him call out:

"Marie-Rose!"

She instantly rose and hastened to meet him.

Brigadier Frederick

They kissed each other and returned laughing, arm in arm. I was pleased and said to myself :

" They love each other dearly. They are good children."

Old grandmother Anne, who was nearly always shut up in her own room, was looking too, leaning out of the little window surrounded with ivy, with her eyelids puckered up, her old face wrinkled with satisfaction ; she called me :

" Frederick !"

" What is it, grandmother ? "

" I am growing young as at the time of my own marriage. It was the year of the comet in which they made such good wine before the great Russian winter ; you have heard them talk of that, Frederick ; all our soldiers were frozen."

" Yes, grandmother."

She liked to recall those old stories, and we did not think that we should soon see the same things.

The good people of Phalsbourg, the poorest, such as father Maigret, old Paradis, grandfather Lafougére, all of them old soldiers without any means of subsistence but public charity and their medal of St. Helena, began to come to look for mushrooms in the woods ; they knew all the different kinds from the small to the large Polish mushroom ; they gathered also strawberries and mulberries. The wood strawberries, which are the best, sell in the town for two *sous* a quart, mushrooms for three *sous* the small basketful.

The lower meadow, by the river bank, gave them also quantities of salad. How many times those poor old backs were forced to stoop in order to earn a *sou !*

And every year we received orders to enforce the forest laws more severely, to prevent the poor from picking up the dead leaves and beech nuts, which was as much as to say to "prevent them from living."

Things went on this way till the hay-making season, when came the great drought ; it lasted till the end of July, and we feared for the potatoes.

As to the *plebiscite*, I won't talk to you about that ; those things did not worry us foresters much. One fine morning we received the order to go to the Petite Pierre, and all the brigade, after assembling at my house, left together in their holiday clothes to vote ; yes, as we had been ordered to do. Then, stopping at the inn of the Three Pigeons, we drank a bumper to the Emperor's health, after which every one went home and never thought of it any more.

Brigadier Frederick

The people complained of but one thing at Graufthal, Dôsenheim, and Echbourg, and that was the lack of rain. But in the depths of the valleys dry weather was always the most beautiful and the richest; we never lacked moisture; the grass grew in abundance, and all the birds in Alsace, blackbirds, thrushes, bullfinches, and wood pigeons, with their young nestlings, enjoyed themselves with us as if in an aviary.

It was also the best time one could wish for fishing, for when the waters were low all the trout ascended to the springs beneath the rocks, where one could take them out in one's hand.

You may well believe that there was no lack of fishermen. Marie-Rose had never before had as many omelettes and fried dishes to prepare. She superintended everything and answered the compliments made to her upon her approaching marriage without stopping her work. She looked as fresh as a rose; merely looking at her, Jean Merlin's eyes grew moist with tenderness.

Who would have imagined at that time that we were going to have a war with the Prussians? What interest had we in that? Beside, did not every one say that the *plebiscite* had been voted to keep peace? Such an idea had never entered our heads, when, one July evening, the little Jew,

David, who had been to Dôsenheim to buy a calf, said to me as he passed :

"You have heard the great news, brigadier ?"

"No ; what is it ?"

"Well, the Paris newspapers say that the Emperor is about to declare war upon the King of Prussia."

I could not believe it, because the wood-merchant Schatner, who had returned a few days before from Sarrebrück, had told me that the country thereabouts was swarming with troops, cavalry, infantry, artillery, and that even the citizens had their knapsacks, their guns, and their complete outfits, ticketed and numbered, all arranged in good order on shelves in large barracks, and that at the first sign of the *hauptmann* these people would have nothing to do but to dress themselves, receive cartridges, get into a railway car, and fall upon our backs *en masse.* As for us, we had nothing at all, either in our towns or our villages, so simple good sense made me think that they would not declare war on these Germans before having put us in a condition to defend ourselves.

So I shrugged my shoulders when the Jew told me such an absurd thing, and I said :

"Do you take the Emperor for a fool ?"

But he went off, dragging his calf by the rope, and saying :

"Wait a bit, brigadier; you will see—this won't last long."

All that he could say on that score came to the same thing, and when Jean Merlin came that evening, as usual, it never occurred to me to tell him about it.

Unfortunately, eight or ten days later, the thing was certain ; they were calling in all soldiers away on leave of absence. It was even stated that the Bavarians had cut the telegraph wires in Alsace—that innumerable troops were passing Saverne, and that others were encamped at Niederbronn.

XI

ALL at once it was rumoured that there had been fighting near Wissembourg, and that same evening the inhabitants of Neu Willer, fleeing with their furniture piled on carts to Lutzelstein, told us at the very door of the house, without daring to come in, that several of our battalions had been slaughtered ; that the general of the vanguard had been left on the field ; that Wissem-

bourg was in flames, and that our troops were
retiring towards Bitche.

These people seemed bewildered with terror;
instead of continuing on their way to Petite
Pierre, the idea struck them all at once that it
was not strongly enough fortified, and in spite
of the circuit of three leagues that they had
just made, the whole band, men and women,
began to climb the Falberg hill to fly to Strasbourg.

Then desolation reigned among us. Merlin
and his mother came to our house to talk over the
bad news. The grandmother lamented. As for
me, I said there was no need to be cast down
about it, that the Germans would never dare to
risk themselves in our forests; that they did not
know the roads, and other reasons like that, which
did not prevent me from being very uneasy myself, for all that Captain Rondeau had said to us
one year before came back to me; the wood-cutters that he had caused to be arrested at Lutzelstein rose before my eyes; and then I was humili-
ated to think that the soldiers of Baden and Bavaria had beaten the French at their first encounter.
I knew that they were ten to one, but that did
not lessen my grief.

It was our first bad night. I could not sleep,

and I heard Marie-Rose, in her little side room, get up, open the window, and look out.

All outside was as silent as if nothing had happened; not a leaf was stirring, so calm was the air; some crickets were chirping on the ground, which was still warm six hours after sunset, and along the river the frogs were uttering their long, drawn-out cry.

My inward emotion prevented me from sleeping. About four o'clock Ragot began to bark down-stairs; some one was knocking at the door. I dressed myself, and two minutes after, went down to open the door.

A man, the younger Klein-Nickel, of Petite Pierre, brought me an order from Inspector Laroche to come without delay.

Marie-Rose had come down-stairs. I only waited long enough to snatch a morsel, and then I left with my gun slung over my shoulder. By seven o'clock I was at M. Laroche's door, and I went in. The inspector was seated at his desk writing.

"Ah! it is you, Frederick," he said, laying down his pen, "take a seat. We have had some pretty bad news; you know that our little body of men detached for observation has had a misfortune?"

"Yes, sir."

"They allowed themselves to be surprised," said he; "but that is nothing; it will not occur again."

He appeared as tranquil as usual, and said that in every war there were ups and downs; that a first unfortunate engagement did not signify anything, but that it was always good to take precautions in view of more serious events impossible to foresee; consequently, that it was necessary to tell all the men of my brigade, and those that we were employing on the forest roads, to be ready to march with their pickaxes, hatchets, and shovels, at the first order, because it would perhaps be necessary to blow up the rocks and to cut the roads by means of ditches and the felling of trees.

"You understand," said he, seeing me rather uneasy, "that these things are simply measures of forethought, nothing is threatening; Marshal Mac-Mahon is concentrating his troops near Hagenau; everything is in movement; there is nothing immediate to fear; but the chief thing is to be ready in case of need; when everything is ready, we will act rapidly and surely. I may receive an order from General de Failly to block the roads, and in such a case the order must be executed within a few hours."

" It will not take long, sir," I answered; " everywhere the rocks are leaning over the roads; in falling they would take everything with them to the bottom of the valley."

" Exactly," said he. " But, first, every one must be warned. We have no lack of blasting powder; if the order arrives, all my colleagues having taken the same measures, it will be a day's journey from Bitche to Dabo; not a cannon, not an ammunition wagon can pass from Alsace to Lorraine."

He said this as he accompanied me to the door, and shook hands with me.

As I was going thoughtfully home, I saw on the height of Altenberg some soldiers who were planting stockades along the hillside. The greatest confusion was reigning in the suburbs, people were running from house to house to get news, two or three companies of infantry were encamped in a potato-field.

All that day and the next I did nothing but carry the orders of the inspector from Frohmühle to Echbourg, from Echbourg to Hangsviller, to Graufthal, to Metting, etc., telling each of what he would have to do, the places where we were to meet, the rocks which we were to attack.

On the third day I came home, so worn out

that I could not eat nor even sleep for several hours. However, towards morning I fell into a heavy sleep, from which I was roused by Marie-Rose coming into my room and opening the window towards Dösenheim.

"Listen, father," said she, in a trembling voice; "listen to that noise. What is it? We hear nothing but that in the whole valley."

I listened. It was an endless booming that filled the mountain, and at times covered the noise of the wind in the trees. It did not take me long to understand what it meant, and I answered:

"It is cannon. They are fighting seven or eight leagues from here, near Woerth. It is a great battle."

Marie-Rose instantly ran down-stairs, and after having dressed myself I followed her into the lower room, where the grandmother was also; her chin trembled as she looked at me with wide-open eyes.

"It is nothing," I told them; "do not be afraid; whatever happens, the Germans will never come this far; we have too many good places to defend our passes."

But I was very far from feeling very confident myself.

The cannonading grew louder, sometimes like

the distant rolling of a storm ; then it died away, and we heard nothing more but the rustling of the leaves, the barking of Ragot before the door, and the quacking of a duck among the willows by the river. These voices of the solitude, when one thought of what was going on behind the curtain of the forest, had something strange about them.

I should have liked to climb the rocks to see at least what was going on on the other side, in the plain ; but as the order to commence operations might arrive at any minute, I was forced to stay where I was.

This went on till three o'clock in the afternoon.

I walked about, trying to put a brave face on the matter, so as not to frighten the women. This day, the sixth of August, was very long ; even to-day, when so many other griefs have overwhelmed us, I cannot think of it without a heavy heart.

The most terrible moment was, when all at once the dull sound that we had heard since morning ceased. We listened at the garden window, but not a breath, not a sound but those from the valley reached us. It was only after a few minutes that I said :

" It is over. The battle is ended. Now some

are running away and the others are pursuing them. God grant that we have conquered."

And till night not a soul appeared in the neighbourhood. After supper we went to bed with heavy hearts.

XII

THE next day was very gloomy; the sky was cloudy, and at length it began to rain, after the two months' drought; the rain fell heavily and continuously; the hours passed slowly away, the order to commence operations did not come, and I said to myself:

"That is a good sign! So much the better! If we had been defeated the order would have arrived early this morning."

But we had no news, and about three o'clock, losing patience, I said to Marie-Rose and the grandmother:

"See here, I cannot stand this any longer; I must go to Petite Pierre to find out what is going on."

I put on my water-proof cape and went out into the pouring rain. On our sandy soil the water flows off without soaking into the ground. I arrived at *Petite-Pierre*, where every one was then shut up in the cottages, about six o'clock. At the point of the fort, high up in air a sentinel was on guard outside of his watch-box.

A few minutes later I entered the office of the chief inspector. He was there alone, walking up and down with a bowed back and a gloomy air, and when I raised my hood he stopped short and said to me :

"It is you, Father Frederick, is it? Have you come to hear the news and to get your orders?"

"Yes, sir," I replied.

"Well, the news is bad ; the battle is lost ; we are repulsed from Alsace, and one hundred and fifty thousand Germans are advancing to enter Lorraine."

A cold shiver ran down my back, and as he said no more I murmured :

"Everything is ready, sir ; there is nothing to do but to distribute the powder for the mines and to commence felling the trees ; we are all ready and waiting."

Then, smiling bitterly and running his hands through his thick brown hair, he cried :

"Yes, yes, we are all like that. Time presses ; the retreat is continuing by Bitche and Saverne, the enemy is sending out scouts in all directions, and the orders do not come."

I answered nothing, and then, seating himself, he cried :

"After all, why should I hide the truth from you ? General de Failly has sent me word that the abattis are useless, and that there is nothing for us to do."

I was as though rooted to the ground and a cold trembling shook my limbs. The inspector recommenced his walk with his hands crossed behind his back under the skirts of his coat, and as he paced to and fro, without saying another word, I added :

"And now, what are we to do, sir ?"

"Remain at your posts like brave fellows," he said. "I have no other orders to give you."

Something choked me ; he saw that, and, looking at me with moistened eyes, he held out his hand to me, saying :

"Come, Father Frederick, take courage. After all, it is pleasant to be able to say, a hand upon the heart, ' I am a brave man ! ' That is *our* recompense."

And I said, deeply moved :

"Yes, sir, yes, that is all which remains to us, and that will never be lacking."

He did me the honour to accompany me down

the walk to the gate, and again pressing my hand, he cried :

"Courage ! courage !"

Then I set off again, descending the great valley. The rain covered the pool of the Fromühle, which was quivering all gray among the willows and the parched herbage.

As to telling you about the ideas which chased each other through my head, and how often I passed my hand over my face to wipe away the tears and the rain which were flowing from it—as to relating to you that, George, it is not in my power; that would take a wiser man than I ; I felt myself no longer, I did not know myself, and I repeated to myself in my trouble :

"No orders—it is useless. The general says that it is useless to cut down the trees and to block up the roads. Then he wants the enemy to advance and to come through the passes."

And I marched on.

It was dark night when I reached the house. Marie-Rose was waiting for me, seated by the table ; she observed me with an anxious eye, and she seemed to ask, "What has happened—what orders have we."

But I said nothing, and, throwing my cape, all

streaming with rain, on the back of a chair, and shaking my cap, I cried :

"Go to bed, Marie-Rose, we will not be disturbed to-night ; go and sleep tranquilly ; the general at Bitche does not want us to stir. The battle is lost, but we will have another in Alsace, at Saverne, or farther off, and the roads are to remain open. We have no need to do anything, the roads will be well guarded."

I do not know what she thought about it, but at the end of a minute, seeing that I did not sit down, she said :

"I have kept your soup near the fire, and it is still hot if you would like something to eat, father."

"Bah ! I am not hungry," I answered ; "let us go to bed : it is late, and that is the best thing to do."

I could no longer restrain myself ; anger was gaining upon me. I went out and bolted the door, and then taking the lamp I went up-stairs. Marie-Rose followed me, and we each went to our own room.

I heard my daughter go to bed, but I remained thinking for a long time, leaning my elbows on the table and watching the little yellow light before the black panes where the ivy leaves were shivering in the rain, winking my eyes and saying to my-self :

" Frederick, there are, nevertheless, many asses in the world, and they do not walk in the rear ; they march in front and lead the others."

At last, as the night advanced towards two o'clock, thinking that it was useless to burn oil for nothing, I undressed and went to bed, blowing out my lamp.

On that very night of the seventh to the eighth of August, the Germans, having reconnoitred to a great distance and finding that all the roads were free, advanced in a body and took possession of the passes, not only of La Zingel but also of La Zorn, thus investing Phalsbourg, the bombardment of which was begun two days later.

They passed also into Lorraine by the great tun-nel of Homartin, while our army fell back, by forced marches, upon Nancy, and finally upon Chalons.

Thus the two great German armies of Woerth and Forbach found themselves united, and all others were as if swallowed up, cut off from all help and even from all hope.

You can easily picture to yourself that immense army of Prince Frederick ; Bavarians, Wurtem-burgers, Badeners, cavalry, artillery, infantry, which defiled by squadrons and by regiments through our lovely valley; that torrent of human beings which goes on and on, ever forward, without interruption during a whole week, and the cannon which thunders around the place, and the old rocks of the Graufthal which resound with echoes upon echoes, and then the smoke of the conflagration which arises to Heaven forming a sombre dome above our valleys.

XIII

AFTER the grand passage of the German army and the bombardment of the city, thousands of *landwehr* came to occupy the country. These people filled up all the villages and hamlets; here one company, there two; further on three or four, commanded by Prussian officers. They guarded all the roads and paths, they made requisitions of all kinds: bread, wheat, flour, hay, straw, cattle, nothing came amiss to them; they amused themselves at the corner of the fire, talked of their wives and children with an air of tender emotion, pitied the fate of their poor brothers of Alsace and Lorraine, and sighed over our misery. But all that did not prevent them from eating and drinking heartily at our expense, and from stretching themselves out in the old arm-chair of the grandmother

neighbourhood, and that preserved us from visits from that good race which wished us so much good.

It was also said that the members of the forest guard would be kept, that the salary of the old guards would even be augmented, and that several would obtain promotion.

You can understand my indignation when I heard such things said; I had not forgotten the advice of our good Chief Inspector; I reminded our men of it at every opportunity:

"We must stay at our posts! Perhaps the luck will not always be against us. Let every one do his duty till the end. I have no other orders to give you."

He observed this order himself, staying at Petite Pierre and continuing to fulfil the duties of his office.

Strasbourg was defending itself; there was fighting going on round Metz. From time to time I sent Merlin to get the orders from our superiors, and the answer was always: "Nothing is hopeless. We may be called upon at any minute. Let every one stay where he is!"

We waited then, and the autumn, always so beautiful in our mountains, with its russet leaves, its silent forests, where the song of birds was no longer heard; its meadows newly mown and smooth as a carpet as far as the eye could reach; the river covered with gladiols and dead leaves, this great spectacle so calm at all times, was still grander and sadder than ever in the midst of the terrible events through which we were passing.

How often then, listening to the endless murmur of the forest, over which was passing the first cold shiver of the winter, how often have I said to myself :

"While you are looking, Frederick, at those old woods wherein everything is sleeping, what is happening down yonder in Champagne? What has become of that immense army, the cavalry, the infantry, the cannons, all those thousands of beings going eagerly to destruction for the glory and interest of a few? Shall we see them driven back in disorder? Will they remain lying amid the mists of the Meuse, or will they return to place their heel upon our necks?"

I imagined great battles. The grandmother also was very uneasy; she sat by the window and said:

"Listen, Frederick, do you hear nothing?"

And I listened; it was only the wind among the dry leaves.

Sometimes, but rarely, the city seemed to

awake; so a few cannon shots thundered amid the echoes from Quatre Vents to Mittelbroun and then all was silent again. The idea of Metz sustained us; it was from there, above all, that we hoped to obtain succour.

I have nothing more to tell you about this autumn of 1870; no news, no visits, and towards the last but little hope.

But I must tell you now about a thing that surprised us a good deal, that we could not understand, and which unhappily has now become too clear for us, like many other things.

XIV

ABOUT two weeks after the establishment of Bismark Bohlen at Hagenau, we saw arrive one morning in the valley a vehicle similar to those used by the Germans who were starting for America before the invention of railroads—a long wagon, loaded with hundreds of old traps, straw beds, bedsteads, frying-pans, lanterns, etc., with a muddy dog and an unkempt wife and a horde of scabby children, and the master himself leading his sorry jade by the bridle.

We looked at them in amazement, thinking,

Brigadier Frederick

"What does all this mean? What are these people coming to do among us?"

Under the cover near the pole the woman, already old, yellow, and wrinkled, her cap put on awry, was picking the heads of the children, who were swarming in the straw, boys and girls, all light-haired and chubby and pussy, as potato-eaters always are.

"Wilhelm, will you be quiet?" she said. "Wait till I take a look—wait, I see something. Good, I have it; you can tumble about now. Wilhelmina, come put your head upon my knees; each must take their turn; you can look at the pine trees later."

And the father, a big man, in a bottle-green coat, that had a thousand wrinkles in the back; his cheeks hanging, his little nose adorned with a pair of spectacles, his pantaloons tucked into his boots, and a big porcelain pipe in his mouth, pulled on his miserable horse by the bridle and said to his wife:

"Herminia, look at those forests, those meadows, this rich Alsace. We are in the terrestrial paradise."

It was a group resembling the gipsies, and, as Merlin came to see us that day, we talked of nothing but that the whole evening.

Brigadier Frederick

But we were destined to see many more of them, for these strangers, in old *cabriolets*, basket wagons, *chars-a-banc*, and two or four wheeled carriages, put into requisition along the road, continued to pass for a long time. From the first of them, the remembrance of whom has remained in my mind, the train was never ending; there passed daily three, four, or five vehicles, loaded with children, old men, young women, and young girls— the last gotten up in an odd style, with dresses which, it seemed to me, I remembered having seen some fifteen or twenty years before upon the ladies of Saverne, and with wide hats, trimmed with paper roses, set ɩpon their plaits, just three hairs thick, like the *queues* of our grandfathers.

These people talked all kinds of German and were hard to understand. They had also all kinds of faces: some broad and fat, with venerable beards; others sharp as a knife-blade, and with their old overcoats buttoned to the throat, to hide their shirts; some with light gray eyes and stiff, shaggy, red whiskers; others little, round, lively, going, running, and wriggling about; but all, at the sight of our beautiful valley, uttering cries of admiration and lifting up their hands, men, women, and children, as we are told the Jews did on entering into the Promised Land.

Thus came these people from all parts of Germany; they had taken the railroads to our frontiers, but all our lines being then occupied by their troops and their provision and ammunition trains starting from Wissembourg or from Soreltz, they were forced to travel in wagons, after the Alsatian fashion.

Sometimes one and sometimes another would ask us the way to Saverne, Metting, or Lutzelstein; they got down at the spring below the bridge and drank from one of their pans or from the hollow of their hands.

Every day these passages were repeated, and I cudgelled my brain to find out what these foreigners were coming to do among us at so troubled a time, when provisions were so scarce and when we did not know to-day what we should have to eat the morrow. They never said a word, but went upon their way, under the protection of the *landwehr* which filled the country. We have since learned that they shared in the requisitions—a fact which permitted them to save money and even to get themselves into good condition on the road.

George, all these Bohemians of a new species, whose miserable air filled our hearts with pity, even in the midst of our troubles, were the functionaries which Germany sent to be our administrators and

Brigadier Frederick

our rulers, preceptors, controllers, notaries, school-masters, foresters, etc. They were persons who, from the months of September and October, long before the treaty of peace was signed, arrived tranquilly to take the place of our own people, saying to them, without ceremony, " Get out of there, so that I may get in."

One would have said that it was all agreed upon beforehand, for it happened so even before the capitulation of Strasburg.

How many poor devils, beer barrels or schnaps drinkers, who had been whipping the devil around the stump for years and years in all the little cities of Pomerania, of Brandenburg, and further still, who never would have become anything at home, and who did not know from whom to ask for credit at home for rye bread and potatoes—how many such men fell then upon rich Alsace, that terrestrial paradise, promised to the Germans by their kings, their professors, and their school-masters !

At the time of which I speak they were still modest, notwithstanding the wonderful victories of their armies; they were not yet sure of preserving that extraordinary good-fortune to the end, and, comparing their old tattered coats and their miserable appearance with the easy fortune of the

least of the functionaries of Alsace and of Lorraine, they doubtless said to themselves :

" It cannot be possible that the Lord should
have chosen scamps like us to fill such good places.
What extraordinary merit have we, then, to play
first fiddle in a country such as this, which the
French have occupied for two hundred years,
which they have cultivated, planted, and enriched
with workshops and factories and improvements
of all kinds ? Provided that they do not return
to retake it, and to force us to return to our
schnaps and our potatoes."

Yes, George, with a little common sense and
justice, these intruders must have reasoned thus
to themselves ; a sort of uneasiness could be recognised in their eyes and in their smile. But once
Strasburg was taken and Metz given up, and they
comfortably installed in large and fine houses,
which they had not built, sleeping in the good
beds of prefects, under-prefects, judges, and other
personages, of whom they had never even had
an idea; after having imposed taxes upon the
good lands which they had not sowed, and laid
hands upon the registers of all the administrations,
which they had not established, seeing the money,
the good money of rich Alsace, flowing into their
coffers—then, George, they believed themselves

to be really presidents of something, inspectors, controllers, receivers, and the German pride, which they know so well how to hide with cringing when they are not the stronger—that brutal pride puffed out their cheeks.

There always remained to them during the time that I was still down yonder an old remembrance of the Lorempé Strasse and of the Speingler Volk, where they had formerly lived. That remembrance made them very economical; two of them would order a mug of beer and pay for it between them; they disputed about farthings with the shoemaker and the tailor; they found something to find fault with in every bill, crying out that we wanted to cheat them; and the poorest cobbler among us would have been ashamed to display the meanness of these new functionaries, who promised us so many benefits in the name of the German fatherland, and who showed us so much avarice and even abominable meanness. But that only showed us with what race we had now to do.

Brigadier Frederick

XV

ONE day, towards the end of October, one of the *gens-d'armes* of Bismark Bohlen, who passed every morning through the valley, halted at the door of the forest house, calling :

" Hillo, somebody !" I went out.

" You are the Brigadier Frederick ?" asked the man.

" Yes," I answered, " my name is Frederick, and I am a brigadier forester."

" All right," said he, holding out a letter ; " here is something for you."

Then he trotted off to join his comrade, who was waiting for him a little farther on. I entered the house. Marie-Rose and the grandmother were uneasy ; they looked on in silence as I opened the letter, saying :

" What can those Prussians want with me ? "

It was an order from the Oberförster,* established at Zornstadt, to be at his house the next day, with all the foresters of my brigade. I read the letter aloud and the women were frightened.

" What are you going to do, father ?" asked Marie-Rose, after a pause.

" That is what I am thinking about," I an-

* Chief Inspector of the forest.

84

swered ; "these Germans have no right to give me orders, but they are now the strongest ; they may turn us out of doors any day. I must think it over."

I was walking up and down the room, feeling very much worried, when all at once Jean Merlin passed rapidly before the windows, ascended the steps and entered.

"Good morning, Marie-Rose," said he, "good morning, grandmother. You have received the order from the Oberförster, brigadier ? "

"Yes."

"Ah !" said he, "those people have no confidence in us ; all the foresters have received the same thing. Shall we go ? "

"We must see about it," I said ; "you must go to Petite Pierre and ask the advice of our inspector."

The clock was striking eight. Jean started at once ; at twelve o'clock he had already returned to tell us that M. Laroche wished us to see what the Germans wanted with us, and to send him an account of it as soon as possible. So it was resolved that we should go.

You must know, George, that since the arrival of the Germans the forests were robbed by wholesale ; all the wood still in cords and piled in the clearings, vanished, fagot by fagot : the *landwehr* carried off all that was within their reach ; they liked to sit by a good fire in their earthworks before the city. The peasants, too, helped themselves liberally, one might almost say that the property of the State belonged to the first-comer.

I told my guards without ceasing to watch the culprits closely, that the wood still belonged to France, and that after the war they would have to account for it. My district suffered less than the others, because I continued to make my rounds as heretofore ; people always respect those who do their duty.

So I sent Jean to tell his comrades to meet without fail the next day at the forest house, wearing their uniform, but without badges, and that we would go together to Zornstadt.

The next day, when all had assembled, we took up the line of march, and about one o'clock we arrived in the vestibule of the great house, wherein the Oberförster had installed himself and all his family. It was a great holiday at Zornstadt for the Prussians. They had just heard of the capitulation of Bazaine, and they were singing in all the public houses. The Oberförster was giving a banquet. Naturally this ill news made our hearts very heavy. The other brigades had already met at the door, headed by the brigadiers, Charles Werner, Jacob Hepp, and Balthazar Redig.

After having shaken hands, it was decided that we should listen to the remarks of the Ober-förster in silence, and that I, as the oldest briga-dier, should speak for all if there was anything to reply. We still waited for over half an hour, as the banquet was not yet over ; they were laughing and joking, playing the piano and singing " Die Wacht am Rhein." In spite of their immense vanity, these people had not expected such great victories, and I think that if we had had other generals, that, in spite of their preparations and their superiority in numbers, they would not have had the opportunity to be so merry at our ex-pense.

At last, about two o'clock, a German in a green felt hat, adorned with two or three cock feathers, with a joyous air, and cheeks scarlet to the ears, for he had just left the kitchen, came and opened the door, saying :

" You may come in."

After traversing a long room, we found the Oberförster alone, seated in an arm-chair at the end of a long table, still covered with dessert and bottles of all kinds, with a red face, and his hands crossed upon his stomach with an air of satisfaction. He was a handsome man in his jacket of green cloth edged with marten fur—yes, George, I will confess it, a very handsome man, tall, well-made, a square head, short hair, solid jaws, long red mustaches and side whiskers, that, so to speak, covered his shoulders. Only his large red nose, covered with flowery splotches, astonished you at first sight, and forced you to turn away your eyes out of respect for his rank. He looked at us as we entered, his little gray eyes screwed up ; and when we had all gathered round the table, cap in hand, after having scrutinized us carefully, he settled his waistcoat, coughed a little, and said to us, with an air of deep emotion :

"You are good people. You have all honest German faces ; that pleases me ! Your get-up is very good also ; I am satisfied with you !"

In the side room the guests were laughing ; this forced the Oberförster to interrupt himself :

"Wilhelm, shut the door !" said he to the servant who had let us in. The waiter obeyed, and the Oberförster continued :

"Yes, you have good German faces ! When I think that you have been kept for so many years in the service of that race of boasters, it makes me angry. But, thanks to the Almighty, and thanks also to the armies of our glorious King William,

the hour of deliverance has arrived, the reign of
Sodom and Gomorrah is over. We will no longer
see honest fathers of families doing their duty with
loyalty and exactness, and preserving the property
of his Majesty ; we will no longer see such people
living on a salary ⸏f five or six hundred francs, while
adventurers, law-breakers, gamblers, people swallowed up in vice, award themselves forty millions
a year to support dancing girls, cooks, and toadies,
and to declare war at random upon pacific neighbours, without reason, without foresight, without
armies, without ammunition, and without cannon,
like real idiots ! No, that will never be seen
again ; old Germany is opposed to it !"

Then the Oberförster, satisfied with what he
had just said, filled his glass in order to refresh his
ideas ; he drank solemnly, with half-closed eyes,
and continued :

" I have sent for you to confirm you in all your
situations ; for I visited the forests, I saw that all
was in order ; I saw that you were faithful servants ; it is but just that you should remain. And
I announce to you that your salaries are to be
doubled ; that old servants, instead of being put
on the retired list, shall receive promotion ; that
they shall enjoy an honest competency proportion-
ate to their rank ; finally, that the munificence of

his Majesty will extend itself to you all, and in your old age you will bless the happy annexation of this noble land, Alsace, to the mother country. You will relate some day to your children and grandchildren the story of this long captivity in Babylon, during which you suffered so much, and you will also become the most faithful subjects of his Most Gracious Majesty, the King of Prussia. This is what I wish! Old functionaries like you, honoured and respected in the country because of the faithfulness of their services, exercise always a great influence over the peasantry. You will express loudly your attachment to our glorious King William, that hearty attachment which every German feels. Yes, you will take the oath of allegiance to his Majesty; and as to the rest, as to the augmentation of your salary, I give you my word as an Oberförster that all will be done according to the promises I have just made you."

While he was talking he did not cease to watch us; behind us were two or three tall Germans in uniform, who appeared dazzled and touched by his discourse. But as for us we remained cold, cap in hand; and as I was to be the spokesman they all looked at me to see what I thought.

You can imagine, George, my silent indignation to see that they called us good servants, honest people in order to make traitors of us. I felt my cheeks getting red; I would have liked to be able to answer that only rascals would have accepted the title of honest men, by forfeiting their honour; but I held my tongue, not wishing to answer for my comrades, several of whom had large families; the responsibility seemed too great.

The Oberförster having ended, he looked at us fixedly; at me in particular, and he said:

"Well! you may speak; I authorize you to speak."

Then I answered:

"Sir, as the oldest forester of the three brigades, my comrades have requested me to speak for them all; but the proposition that you have just made is serious; I think that every one will ask for time to think it over."

They all nodded assent; and he, who was really astonished, for he had doubtless thought that the augmentation of the salaries would decide everything, remained for over a minute with his eyes wide open, staring at me as if I were something extraordinary; then he did as much for the others, and, frowning, he said gruffly:

"I give you twenty-four hours! To-morrow at this time I want to have your written reply, signed by each of you; yes or no! Do not think that there is any lack of men, there are plenty in Germany, good people, old foresters, who know the service as well as the smartest of you, who would ask nothing better than to come into this rich Alsace, where everything grows so abundantly, to live in comfortable houses in the midst of magnificent forests, having nothing to do but to take a little turn in the neighbourhood morning and evening, to draw up a report, and to receive for that twelve or fifteen hundred francs a year, with the garden, the strip of meadow, the pasture for the cow, and all the rest of it. No, do not think that ! Hundreds are waiting impatiently till we tell them to come. And weigh well your answer ; think of your wives and your children ; beware of having to repent bitterly if you say no ! France is completely ruined, she is penniless ; the wretched forests that are left her in Brittany and the Landes are nothing but broom-sticks ; the guards of these thickets will retain their places, and you will never get other situations. You are Germans. The French used you and despised you ; they called you blockheads ! Think over all this ; it is the advice of an honest man that I give you, of a German brother and the father of a family !"

He looked at me, thinking that I was going

to say something; but I compressed my lips, and I felt as if little puffs of cold wind were passing over my forehead. All my companions were also silent. At one side behind the door some one was playing on the piano, and a woman was singing a sweet and melancholy little song.

"Twenty-four hours," he repeated, rising; "not another minute." And, throwing his napkin on the table angrily, he added:

"Remember, too, that those who wish to answer *no* can pack up at once; the highway is open to them. We will never keep enemies among us —dangerous persons—that would be too stupid. We are not Frenchmen."

So he entered the next room, while we went out by the vestibule.

What the Oberförster had said to us, "that we would have a hard time getting situations in France, and that the Germans would force us to be off without mercy," was terrible; the most courageous hung their heads.

Some of them, very pale, were thinking of going to the Fir Tree Inn to deliberate; they wanted, above all, to know my opinion; but I said, stopping before the door of the inn:

"From this time, comrades, let us economize all the little money that we have; five *sous* for a

glass of wine is always five *sous*. We shall probably have to break up housekeeping, and at these
unhappy times everything is dear ; travelling costs
money when we take women, children, and old
men with us."

Big Kern insisted upon knowing what I
thought ; several of them gathered around me,
so I finally said :

"See here, for what concerns myself I know
what I ought to do ; but at such a moment as
this every one should be free to follow his own
conscience ; I shall give no advice to any one."

And seeing poor Jacob Hepp, the father of
six small children, standing with drooping head,
hanging arms, and cast-down eyes, I said :

"Come! Let us shake hands all round once
more—for the last time, perhaps! May the old
recollections of friendship follow us wherever
Heaven may conduct us."

Several of us kissed each other, and at that
place we parted.

XVI

JEAN MERLIN and I took the road to Felsberg
alone ; I do not know what the others did, whether they entered the inn or returned to their homes.

Brigadier Frederick

As for us, so many ideas were passing through our heads that we walked on for a long while without saying a word.

On leaving Zornstadt, we ascended the hill of Bruyères till we reached the plateau of Graufthal, and suddenly the sun pierced the clouds and shone upon the woods. The sun was very brilliant, and showed us through the leafless trees in the depths of the valley the pretty cottage in which I had passed so many happy days since Father Burat had given me his daughter in marriage.

I stopped short. Jean, who was following me along the path, also halted ; and, leaning on our sticks, we looked for a long time as if in a dream. All the by-gone days seemed to pass before my eyes.

The little cottage, on this clear, cold day, looked as if it were painted on the hillside, in the midst of the tall fir trees ; its roof of gray shingles, its chimney, from which curled a little smoke, its windows, where in summer Marie-Rose placed her pots of pinks and mignonette, the trellis, over which climbed the ivy, the shed and its worm-eaten pillars—all were there before me, one might have thought it possible to touch them.

When I saw that I said to myself :

Brigadier Frederick

"Look, Frederick, look at this quiet corner of the world, wherein thy youth has passed, and from which thou must go away gray-headed, without knowing where to turn; that humble dwelling wherein thy dear wife Catherine gave thee several children, some of whom lie beside her in the earth at Dôsenheim. Look! and remember how calmly thy life has glided away in the midst of worthy people who called thee good son, kind father, and honest man, and prayed God to load thee with blessings. What good does it do thee now to have been a good father and a dutiful son, to have always done thy duty honestly, since they drive thee away, and not a soul can intercede for thee? The Germans are the strongest, and strength is worth more than the right established by God himself."

I trembled at having dared to raise my reproaches to the Almighty, but my grief was too deep, and the iniquity appeared to me to be too great. May Heaven forgive me for having doubted of His goodness.

As to the rest my resolution was taken; I would rather a thousand times have died than have committed so base an action. And, looking at Merlin, who was leaning gloomily against a birch tree near me, I said:

Brigadier Frederick

"I am looking at my old abode for the last time; to-morrow the Oberförster will receive my answer, and day after to-morrow the furniture will be piled upon the cart. Tell me now what do you mean to do?"

Then he flushed scarlet and said: "Oh! Father Frederick, can you ask me that? You pain me by doing so. Do you not know what I will do? I will do like you; there are not two ways of being an honest man."

"That is right—I knew it," I said; "but I am very glad to have heard you say so. Everything must be clear between us. We are not like Germans, who chase the devil round the stump, and think that everything is right, provided it succeeds. Come, let us walk on, Jean, and keep up your courage."

XVII

WE began to descend the hill, and I confess to you, George, that when I approached the house and thought of how I should have to announce the terrible news to my daughter and the grandmother, my legs trembled under me.

At last we reached the threshold. Jean en-

tered first; I followed him and closed the door.
It was about four o'clock. Marie-Rose was peel-
ing potatoes for supper, and the grandmother,
seated in her arm-chair by the stove, was listening
to the crackling of the fire, as she had done for
years past.

Imagine our position. How could we manage to tell them that the Germans were going to
turn us out of doors? But the poor women had
only to look at us to understand that something
very serious had happened.

After having put my stick in the corner by the
clock, and hung my cap on the nail, I walked up
and down the room several times; then, as I had
to commence somehow, I began to relate in detail
the propositions that the Oberförster had made
to us to enter the service of the King of Prussia. I did not hurry myself; I told everything
clearly, without adding or suppressing anything,
wishing that the poor creatures might also have
the liberty of choosing between poverty and shame.

I was sure that they would choose poverty.
Marie-Rose, deadly pale, lifted her hands to Heaven,
murmuring :

" My God! is it possible? Do such rascals
exist in the world? Ah! I would rather die than
join such a company of wretches!"

Brigadier Frederick

It pleased me to see that my daughter had a brave heart, and Jean Merlin was so touched that I saw his lip quiver.

The grandmother seemed to wake up like a snail in its shell; her chin trembled, her dull eyes sparkled with anger; I was surprised at it myself. And when I went on to say that the Oberförster, if we refused to serve Prussia, gave us twenty-four hours to leave our home, her indignation burst forth all at once.

"To quit the house?" said she, lifting her bent form, "but this house is mine! I was born in this house more than eighty years ago, and I have never left it. It was my grandfather, Laurent Duchêne, who first lived here, more than a hundred and thirty years ago, and who planted the fruit trees on the hill; it was my father, Jacquemin, who first marked out the road to Dôsenheim and the paths of Tömenthal; it was my husband, George Burat, and my son-in-law Frederick here, who sowed the first seeds of the beech trees and firs, whose forests now extend over the two valleys; and all of us, from father to son, we have lived quietly in this house; we have earned it; we have surrounded the garden with hedges and palisades; every tree in the orchard belongs to us; we saved up money to buy the meadows, to build the barn

and the stables. Drive us away from this house?
Ah! the wretches! Those are German ideas!
Well, let them come! I, Anne Burat, will have
something to say to them!"

I could not calm the poor old grandmother;
all that she said was just; but with people who
believe that strength is everything, and that shame
and injustice are nothing, what is the use of talking so much?

When she sat down again, all out of breath, I
asked her, in a very sad but firm voice:

"Grandmother, do you wish me to accept service with the Germans?"

"No!" said she.

"Then within forty-eight hours we must all
leave together this old house."

"Never!" she cried. "I will not!"

"And I tell you it must be," said I, with an
aching heart. "I *will* have it so."

"Ah!" she cried, with painful surprise.

And I continued, with anguish:

"You know, grandmother, that I have always
had the greatest respect for you. May those Germans be a thousand times accursed for having
forced me to be disrespectful to you; I hate them
still more for it, if possible! But do you not understand, grandmother, that those brutes are with-

out shame, without honour, without pity even for old age, and if they encountered the slightest resistance they would drag you out by your gray hair? You are weak and they are strong, and that is enough for them! Do you not understand that if I saw such a spectacle I would throw myself upon them, even if they were a regiment, and that they would kill me? Then what would become of you and my daughter? That is what we must think of, grandmother. Forgive me for having spoken so harshly to you, but I do not wish for a minute's grace, nor, I am sure, do you; beside, they would not let us have it, for they are pitiless people!"

She burst into tears and sobbed out:

"Oh! my God! my God! to have to leave this house, where I hoped to see my grand-daughter happy and to nurse my great-grandchildren! My God! why did you not call me away sooner?"

She wept so bitterly that it touched our hearts, and all of us, with bowed heads, felt the tears trickle down our cheeks. How many recollections came to us all! But the poor grandmother had more than any of us, having never quitted the valley for so many years, except to go two or three times a year to market at Saverne or Phalsbourg; those were her longest journeys.

XVIII

AT last the blow was struck. Cruel necessity, George, had spoken by my lips; the women had understood that we must go away, perhaps never to return; that nothing could prevent this fearful misfortune.

That was done; but another duty, still more painful, remained to fulfil. When the lamentations had ceased, and we were meditating, mute and overwhelmed, raising up my voice anew, I said:

"Jean Merlin, you asked me last summer for my daughter in marriage, and I accepted you to be my son, because I knew you, I liked you, and I esteemed you as much as the greatest man in the country. So it was settled; our promises had been given, we wanted nothing more! But then I was a brigadier forester, I was about to receive my pension, and my post was promised to you. Without being rich, I had a little property; my daughter might be considered a good match. Now I am nobody any more; to tell the truth, I am even a poor man. The old furniture I possess suits this house; if it were taken with us it would be in the way; the meadow, for which I paid fifteen hundred francs from my savings, also because it was convenient to the forest house, will be worth little more than half when it has to be sold over again. Beside, perhaps the Germans will declare that all real estate belongs to them. It depends only upon themselves, since the strongest are always in the right! You, too, will find yourself without a situation; you will be obliged to support your old mother. The maintenance of a wife in the midst of all this poverty may appear very troublesome. Therefore, Jean, my honour and that of my daughter oblige me to release you from your promise. Things are no longer as they were; Marie-Rose has nothing, and I can understand that an honest man, on such a grave situation, might change his mind."

Merlin turned pale as he listened to me, and he answered, in a gruff voice:

"I asked for Marie-Rose for her own sake, Father Frederick, because I loved her, and she also loved me. I did not ask for her for the sake of your place, nor yet for the sake of the money she might have; if I had thought of such a thing, I would have been a scoundrel. And now I love her more than ever, for I have seen that she has a noble heart, which is above everything."

And, rising and opening his arms, he cried: "Marie-Rose!"

Brigadier Frederick

Scarcely had he called her, when she turned, her face bathed in tears, and threw herself into his arms. They remained clasped in a close embrace for some time, and I thought to myself :

" All is well ; my daughter is in the hands of an honest man ; that is my greatest consolation in the midst of all my misfortunes."

After that, George, in spite of our grief, we grew calm again. Merlin and I agreed that he would go the next day to carry our answer to Zornstadt : " No, Oberförster, we will not enter the service of the King of Prussia ! " I wrote my letter at once and he put it in his pocket.

It was also agreed that I should go early to Graufthal, and try to find lodgings for ourselves, wherein we could place our furniture. The three first-floor rooms belonging to Father Ykel, the host of the Cup Inn, had been empty ever since the invasion, as not a traveller came to the country. There must certainly be room in his stable, too ; so I hoped to hire them cheap.

As to Merlin, he had still to tell his mother, and he said to us that she would go to Felsberg, where Uncle Daniel would be very glad to receive her. The old schoolmaster and his sister had kept house together for a long time, and it was only after Jean Merlin's installation in the forester's house at Tömenthal that he had taken his mother to live with him. Good old Margredel had nothing to do but to return to the village, where her little house was waiting for her. So our final resolutions were taken.

Jean also took upon himself to go and tell M. Laroche of what had occurred, and to say also that I would come and see him after our flitting. Then he kissed Marie-Rose, said a few encouraging words to the grandmother, and went out. I went with him as far as the threshold and shook hands. The night had come ; it was freezing cold ; every blade of grass in the valley was sparkling with frost, and the sky was glittering with stars. What weather in which to leave our home and to seek another shelter !

As I returned to the room, I saw poor Calas empty the saucepan of potatoes on the table and place the two pots of clotted milk beside the salad-bowl, looking at us with an amazed air ; no one stirred.

"Sit down, Calas," I said ; "eat alone ; none of us are hungry this evening."

So he sat down and began to peel his potatoes ; having cleaned out the stable and given forage to the cattle, he had done his duty and his conscience was easy.

Brigadier Frederick

Happy are those who cannot see the morrow, and whom the Almighty only governs, without kings, without emperors, and without ministers. They have not one-quarter of our sorrows. The squirrel, the hare, the fox, all the animals of the woods and the plains, receive their new fur at the beginning of winter ; the birds of the air receive finer down ; those who cannot live in the snow, for lack of insects to feed them, have strong wings, that enable them to seek a warmer climate.

It is only man who receives nothing ! Neither his labour, nor his foresight, nor his courage can preserve him from misfortune ; his fellow beings are often his worst enemies and his old age is often the extreme of misery. Such is our share of existence.

Some people would like to change these things, but no one has the courage and the good sense which are necessary.

Finally, at nightfall we separated, to think over, each alone in his corner, the terrible blow that had overwhelmed us.

Brigadier Frederick

XIX

ON the following day, which was the first of November, at dawn, I set out for Graufthal. I had put on my blouse, my thick shoes, and my felt hat. The trees along the roadside were bending under their covering of frost ; occasionally a black-bird or a thrush would rise from under the white brushwood, uttering its cry, as if to bid me fare-well. I have often thought of it since ; I was on the path of exile, George ; it was only beginning, and extended very far.

Towards seven o'clock I arrived under the large rocks, where the most wretched huts in the village were situated—the others were built along the banks of the river—and I stopped before that of Father Ykel. I went through the kitchen into the smoky little parlour of the inn. Nothing was stirring ; I thought I was alone and I was about to call, when I saw Ykel, sitting behind the stove, his short black pipe, with a copper cover, between his teeth, and his cotton cap pushed over one ear ; he did not move, as he had had, a few weeks be-fore, an attack of rheumatism, brought on by his long fishing excursions among the mountain streams, and also at night by torchlight, amid the mists.

Brigadier Frederick

The valley had never known such a fisher; he sold crawfish and trout to the great hotels of Strasbourg. Unhappily, as we all have to pay for our imprudences, sooner or later, he had been attacked by the rheumatism, and now all he could do was to sit and think about the best places in the river and the great hauls he used to make.

When I discovered him, his little green eyes were already fixed upon me.

"Is it you, Father Frederick?" he said. "What is your business here among these rascals who are robbing us? If I were you, I would stay quietly in the forest; the wolves are much better neighbours."

"We cannot always do as we like," I answered. "Are your three upper rooms still empty, and have you room enough in your stable for two cows?"

"Haven't I, though!" he cried. "The Prussians have made room! They have taken everything—straw, hay, oats, flour, and the cattle. Ah! room; I guess so; from the garret to the cellar, we have plenty; it will not run out for a long time!"

And he uttered a harsh laugh, gnashing his old teeth and muttering:

"Oh! the wretches! God grant that we may

one day have the upper hand; I would go there on crutches, in spite of my rheumatism, to get back what they took from me!"

"Then," said I, "the rooms are empty?"

"Yes, and the stable, too, with the hayloft. But why do you ask me that?"

"Because I have come to hire them."

"You!" cried he, in amazement. "Then you are not going to stay at the forest house?"

"No, the Prussians have turned me out."

"Turned you out! And why?"

"Because I did not choose to serve under the Germans."

Then Ykel appeared touched; his long hooked nose curved itself over his mouth, and, in a grave voice, he said:

"I always thought you were an honest man. You were a little severe in the service, but you were always just; no one has ever been able to say anything to the contrary."

Then he called:

"Katel! Katel!"

And his daughter, who had just lighted the fire on the hearth, entered.

"Look here, Katel," said he, pointing to me; "here is Father Frederick, whom the Prussians have turned out of his house, with his daughter and grandmother, because he will not join their band. That is a thousand times worse than the requisitions; it is enough to make one's hair stand on end."

His daughter also sided with us, crying that the heavens ought to fall to crush such rascals. She took me up-stairs, climbing the ladder-like stairs to show me the rooms that I wished to hire.

You cannot imagine anything more wretched; you could touch the beams of the ceiling with your hand; the narrow windows, with lead-framed casements, in the shadow of the rocks, gave scarcely a ray of light.

How different from our pretty cottage, so well lighted, on the slope of the hill! Yes, it was very gloomy, but we had no choice; we had to lodge somewhere.

I told Katel to make a small fire in the large room, so as to drive away the damp; then, going down-stairs again, Father Ykel and I agreed that I should have the first floor of his house, two places in the stable for my cows, the little hayloft above, with a pig-sty, one corner of the cellar for my potatoes, and half the shed, where I intended to put the furniture that would not go into the rooms, at a rent of eight francs a month—a pretty large sum at a time when no one was making a *centime.*

Two or three neighbours, the big coal man, Starck, and his wife ; Sophie, the basket-maker ; Koffel, and Hulot, the old smuggler, were then arriving at the inn, to take their glass of brandy, as usual. Ykel told them of the new abominations of the Germans ; and they were disgusted at them. Starck offered to come with his cart and horses to help me to move, and I accepted, thankfully.

Things were settled that way ; Starck promised me again to come without fail before noon ; after which I took the road towards home. It had begun to snow ; not a soul before or behind me was on the path, and, about nine o'clock, I was stamping my feet in the entry to get off the snow.

Marie-Rose was there. I told her briefly that I had engaged our lodgings, that she must prepare the grandmother to leave very soon, to empty the contents of the cupboards into baskets, and to take the furniture to pieces. I called Calas to help me and went to work at once, scarcely taking time enough to breakfast. The hammer resounded through the house ; we heard the grandmother sobbing in the smaller room and Marie-Rose trying to console her.

Brigadier Frederick

It all seems to come back to me. It was terrible to hear the lamentations of the poor old woman, to hear her complain of the fate that overwhelmed her in her old age, and then to call on her husband for aid, good Father Burat, who had died ten years before, and all the old people, whose bones lay in the cemetery at Dôsenheim. It makes me shudder when I think of it, and the kind words of my daughter come back to me and touch my heart anew.

The hammer did its work; the furniture, the little looking-glass by Catherine's bed—my poor dead wife—the portraits of the grandfather and grandmother, painted by Ricard, the same who painted the beautiful signs in the time of Charles X; the two holy-water vessels and the old crucifix, from the back of the alcove; the chest of drawers belonging to Marie-Rose, and the large walnut-wood wardrobe that had come down to us from great-grandfather Duchêne; all those old things that reminded us of people long dead, and of our quiet, peaceful life, and which, for many years, had had their places, so that we could find them by groping in the darkest night; everything was taken away; it was, so to speak, our existence that we had to undo with our own hands!

And Ragot, who came and went, all aston-

ished at the confusion; Calas, who kept asking,
"What have we done, to be obliged to run away
like thieves?" And the rest!—for I do not remember it at all, George! I would even like to
forget it all, and never to have begun this story of
the shame of humanity and the humiliation of
that sort of Christians who reduce their fellow
creatures to utter misery, because they will not
kneel before their pride. However, since we have
begun it, let us go on to the end.

All that was nothing as yet. It was when big
Starck came, and the furniture was loaded on his
wagon, we had at last to tell the grandmother to
leave her little room, and when, seeing all that
desolation in the road, she fell on her face, crying :

"Frederick, Frederick, kill me! let me die,
but do not take me away! Let me, at least,
sleep quietly under the snow in our little garden ! "

Then, George, I wished that I were dead myself. The blood seemed curdling in my veins.
And now, after four years, I would be puzzled to
tell you how the grandmother found herself placed
in the cart, in the midst of the mattresses and
straw beds, under the thousands of snow-flakes
that were falling from the sky.

XX

THE snow, which had continued to fall since morning, was by this time quite deep. The great wagon went slowly on its way, Starck, in front, pulling his nags by the bridle, swearing, and forcing them to advance by blows; Calas, farther on, was driving along the pigs and cows; Ragot was helping him; Marie-Rose and I followed, with drooping heads; and behind us the cottage, all white with snow, among the firs, was gradually vanishing in the distance.

We had still our potatoes, wood, and fodder to take away the next day, so I closed the door and put the key in my pocket before leaving.

At nightfall we arrived before Ykel's house. I took the grandmother in my arms, like a child, and carried her up-stairs to her room, where Katel had kindled a bright fire. Marie-Rose and Katel kissed each other; they had been schoolmates and had been confirmed together at Felsberg. Katel burst into tears. Marie-Rose, who was deadly pale, said nothing. They went up-stairs together, and, while Starck and Calas and two or three of the neighbours were unloading the furniture and putting it under the shed, I went into the parlour, to sit down for a few minutes behind the stove and to take a glass of wine, for I could not stand it any longer; I was exhausted.

Our first night at Graufthal, in that loft, through which poured the draught from the garret, is the saddest that I can remember; the stove smoked, the grandmother coughed in her bed; Marie-Rose, in spite of the cold, got up to give her a drink; the little window-panes rattled at every blast of the wind, and the snow drifted in upon the floor.

Ah! yes, we suffered terribly that first night! And, not being able to close my eyes, I said to myself:

"It will be impossible to live here! We should all be dead in less than two weeks. We must positively go somewhere else. But where shall we go? What road can we take?"

All the villages of Alsace and Lorraine were filled with Germans, the roads were crowded with cannon and convoys; not a hut, not even a stable was free.

These ideas almost made my hair turn gray; I wished that I had broken my neck in coming down the steps of the forest house, and I wished the same thing for the grandmother and my daughter.

Happily, Jean Merlin arrived early the next

morning. He had taken our answer to the Oberförster, he had moved his furniture to Felsberg,
and old Margredel, his mother, was already sitting
quietly beside the fire at Uncle Daniel's house.

He told us that with a good-humoured air,
after having kissed Marie-Rose and said good-
morning to the grandmother.

Only to see how his confidence had already
lightened my heart; and when I complained of
the cold, the smoke, and of our bad night, he
cried:

"Yes! I understand all that, brigadier; I
thought as much; so I hurried to come here.
It is very hard to leave your old ways and come
to live among strangers at your age; that par-
alyzes one's arm. Such occasions change one's
ideas. Here is the key of my cottage and the
book of estimations; you have also your register and the stamping hammer. Well, do you
know what I would do in your place? I would
take everything to our chief inspector, because
the Oberförster of Zornstadt might ask you for
them and force you to give them up. When they
are deposited with M. Laroché no one will have
anything more to say to you. While you are
away Marie-Rose will wash the windows and the
floor; Calas will go with Starck to get the wood,

the fodder, and the potatoes, and I will undertake to arrange the furniture and to put everything in order."

He spoke with so much good sense that I followed his advice. We went down into the large room, and though it is not my habit, we took a good glass of brandy together; after which I set out, the register under my blouse, the hammer in my pocket, and a stout stick in my hand. It was my last journey through the country on affairs connected with the service. The pool of Frohmühle was frozen over; the flour-mill and the saw-mill lower down had ceased to go. No one, since the day before, had followed my path; all seemed desolate; for three hours I did not see a soul.

Then, remembering the smoke from the charcoal kilns, the sound of the wood-cutters' hatchets working in the clearings, lopping the trees, piling up the fagots beside the forest paths, even in midwinter, all that formerly gay life, that profit that gave food and happiness to the smallest hamlets, I said to myself that the robbers, who were capable of troubling such order to appropriate wrongfully the fruit of the labour of others, ought to be hanged.

And from time to time, in the midst of the silence, seeing a sparrow-hawk pass on his large wings, his claws drawn up under his stomach and uttering his war cry, I thought :

"That is like the Prussians ! They have got the Germans in their claws ; they have given them officers who will cudgel them ; instead of working, those people are forced to spend their last penny in the war, and the others have always their beaks and claws in their flesh ; they pluck them leisurely, without their being able to defend themselves. Woe to us all ! The noble Prussians will devour us ; and the Badeners, the Bavarians, the Würtembergers, and the Hessians with us !"

Those melancholy ideas, and many others of the same kind, passed through my mind. About ten o'clock I ascended the stairs of the old fort, abandoned since the beginning of the war ; then descending the Rue du Faubourg, I entered the house of the chief inspector. But the office door in the vestibule at the left was closed ; I rang and tried to open the door, but no one came. I was going out to ask one of the neighbours what had become of M. Laroche, and whether he had been obliged to go away, when an upper door opened, and the chief inspector himself appeared on the stairs in his dressing-gown.

XXI

"Who is there?" said M. Laroche, not recognising me at first under my broad-brimmed felt hat.

"It is I, sir," I answered.

"Ah! it is you, Father Frederick!" said he, quite rejoiced. "Well, come up stairs. All my household has departed, I am here alone; they bring me my meals from the Grapes Inn. Come in, come in!"

We went into a very neat little room on the first floor; a large fire was burning in the stove. And, pushing forward an arm-chair for me:

"Take this chair, Father Frederick," said he, seating himself beside a small table covered with books. So I sat down, and we began to talk over our affairs. I told him about our visit to the Oberförster; he knew all about that and a good many other things beside.

"I am glad to find," said he, "that all our guards, except poor Hepp, the father of six children, have done their duty. With regard to you, Father Frederick, I never had the least doubt about either your son-in-law or yourself."

Then he inquired about our position; and, taking the register and the hammer, he put them in a closet, saying that his papers were already gone, that he would send these after them. He asked me if we were not in pressing need. I answered that I had still three hundred francs, that I had saved to buy a strip of meadow, beside the orchard, that that would doubtless be sufficient."

"So much the better!" said he. "You know, Father Frederick, that my purse is at your service; it is not very full just now; every one has to economize their resources, for Heaven only knows how long this campaign may last; but if you want some money——"

I thanked him again. We talked together like real friends. He even asked me to take a cigar from his box; but I thanked him and refused. Then he asked me if I had a pipe, and told me to light it. I tell you this to make you understand what a fine man our chief inspector was.

I remember that he told me after that that all was not yet over; that doubtless our regular army had surrendered *en masse*; that all our officers, marshals, generals, even the simple corporals had fallen into the power of the enemy, a thing that had never been seen before since the beginning of the history of France, or in that of any other nation; that pained him, and even if I may say so made him indignant. He had tears in his eyes like myself.

But after that, he said that Paris held good, that the great people of Paris had never shown so much courage and patriotism; he added that a large and solid army, though composed of young men, had been formed near Orleans, and that great things were expected from it; that the republic had been proclaimed after Sedan as the peasants go for a doctor when the patient is dying, and that, however, this republic had had the courage to take upon itself the burden of all the disasters, dangers that it had not caused, while those who had drawn us into the war withdrew to a foreign country. That a very energetic man, Gambetta, a member of the provisory government, was at the head of this great movement; that he was calling around him all the Frenchmen in a condition to bear arms, without distinction of opinions, and that if the campaign lasted a few months longer the Germans could not hold out; that all the heads of the families being enlisted, their estates, their workshops, their improvements were neglected. No ploughing or sowing were done, and that the women and children, the entire population, were dying of terrible starvation.

We have since seen, George, that those things

were true; all the letters that we found on the *landwehr* told of the terrible poverty in Germany.

So what M. Laroche told me filled me with hope. He promised also to have my pension paid to me as soon as it would be possible, and about one o'clock I left him, full of confidence. He shook hands with me and called out from the door:

"Keep up a good heart, Father Frederick; we will have happy days yet."

After I left him I felt like another man, and I walked leisurely back to Graufthal, where a most agreeable surprise awaited me.

XXII

JEAN MERLIN had put everything in order. The cracks in the roof and in the doors and windows were stopped up; the floor was washed, the furniture placed and the pictures hung, as much as possible as they were at the forest house. It was bitterly cold outside; our stove, which Jean had put up and blackleaded, drew like a forge bellows, and the grandmother, sitting beside it in her old arm-chair, was listening to the crackling of the fire, and looking at the flame which was lighting up the room. Marie-Rose, with her sleeves rolled up, seemed delighted at my satisfaction; Jean Merlin, his pipe in his mouth and screwing up his eyes, looked at me as if to say:

"Well, Papa Frederick, what do you think of this? Is it cold now in this room? Is not everything clean, shining and in good order? Marie-Rose and I did all that?"

And when I saw all that I said to them:

"All right. The grandmother is warm. Now I see that we can stay here. You are good children!"

That pleased them very much. They set the table. Marie-Rose had made a good soup of cabbages and bacon, for as the Germans took all the fresh meat for their own use we were very glad to get even smoked meat; fortunately potatoes, cabbages, and turnips did not run out and they formed our principal resource.

That evening we all took supper together; and during the repast I related in all its details what the chief inspector had told me about the affairs of the republic. It was the first positive news we had had from France for a long time; so you may guess how eagerly they all listened to me. Jean's eyes sparkled when I spoke of approaching battles near the Loire.

Brigadier Frederick

"Ah!" said he, "they call the French the old soldiers. Indeed! they defend their country, then!"

And I cried, full of enthusiasm:

"Of course, they will defend their country! You had better believe it! The chief inspector says that if it lasts for a few months the others will have enough of it."

Then he twirled his mustache, seemed almost to speak; but then looking at Marie-Rose, who was listening to us with her usual quiet aspect, he went on eating, saying:

"Anyhow, you give me great pleasure by telling me that, Father Frederick; yes, it is famous news."

At last, about eight o'clock, he went away, announcing that he would be back on the morrow or the day after, and we went quietly to bed.

This night was as comfortable as the night before had been cold and disagreeable; we slept soundly in spite of the frost outside.

I had recovered from my sorrow; I thought that we could live at Graufthal till the end of the war.

Brigadier Frederick

XXIII

Once withdrawn under the rocks of Graufthal, I hoped that the Germans would let us alone. What else could they ask from us? We had given up everything; we lived in the most wretched village in the country, in the midst of the forest; their squads came very seldom into this corner, whose inhabitants were so poor that they could scarcely find a few bundles of hay or straw to take away with them. All seemed for the best, and we thought that we would not have anything more to do with the accursed race.

Unfortunately we are often mistaken; things do not always turn out as we thought they would. Soon it was rumoured that Donadien, big Kern, and the other guards had crossed the Vosges; that they were fighting the Germans near Belfort, and all at once the idea struck me that Jean would also want to go. I hoped that Marie-Rose would keep him back, but I was not sure of it. The fear haunted me.

Every morning, while my daughter arranged the rooms, and the grandmother told her beads, I went down stairs to smoke my pipe in the large room with Father Ykel. Koffel, Starck, and others would come dropping in, to take a glass of brandy; they told of domiciliary visits, of orders not to ring the bells, of the arrival of German schoolmasters to replace our own, of the requisitions of all kinds that increased every day, of the unhappy peasants who were compelled to work to feed the Prussians, and of a thousand other atrocities that infuriated one against those stupid Badeners, Bavarians, and Würtembergers, who were allowing themselves to be killed for the sake of King William, and warring against their own interests. Big Starck, who was very pious, and always went to mass every Sunday, said that they would all be damned, without hope of redemption, and that their souls would be burned to all eternity.

That helped to make the time pass agreeably. One day Hulot brought us his grandson, Jean Baptiste, a big boy of sixteen, in his vest and pantaloons of coarse linen, his feet bare, winter as well as summer, in his large shoes, his hair hanging in long, yellow locks over his face, and a satchel hanging over his thin back. This boy, sitting in front of the fire, told us that at Sarrebruck and Landau the *landwehr* were furious; that they were declaiming in all the taverns against the crazy republicans, the cause of all the battles since Sedan, and of the continuation of

the war ; that it had been reported that a battle
had been fought at Coulmiers, near Orleans ; that
the Germans were retreating in disorder, and that
the army of Frederick Charles was going to their
rescue ; but that our young men were also learning to join the army of the republic ; and that the
hauptmänner had laid a fine of fifty francs a day
upon the parents of those who had left the country, which had not prevented him, Jean Baptiste,
from going to the rescue of his country like his
comrades.

Scarcely had he ceased to speak when I ran
up the stairs, four steps at a time, to tell Marie-
Rose the good news. I found her on the landing. She went down to the laundry, and did not
appear in the least astonished.

"Yes, yes, father," she said, "I thought it
would end that way ; every one must lend a
hand—all the men must go. Those Germans
are thieves ; they will return routed and defeated."

Her tranquility astonished me, for the idea
must have occurred to her, too, that Jean, an
able-bodied man, would not stay at home at such
a time, and that he might all at once go off
yonder in spite of his promises of marriage. So
I went to my room to think it over, while she

went down, and two minutes afterward I heard Jean Merlin's step upon the stairs.

He came in quietly, his large felt hat on the back of his head, and he said good‑humouredly :

"Good morning, Father Frederick ; you are alone ?"

"Yes, Jean ; Marie-Rose has just gone to the laundry, and the grandmother is still in bed."

"Ah ! very good," said he, putting his stick behind the door.

I suspected something was coming, from his look. He walked up and down, with bent head, and, stopping suddenly, he said to me :

"You know what is going on near Orleans ? You know that the breaking up of the German army has begun, and that all willing men are called upon. What do you think of it ?"

I flushed scarlet and answered, feeling rather embarrassed :

"Yes, for those on the other side of the Loire it is all very well ; but we others would have a long journey to take, and then the Prussians would arrest us on the road ; they guard all the paths and highways."

"Pshaw !" said he ; "they think the Prussians more cunning than they really are. I would wager that I could pass the Vosges under their noses. Big Kern and Donadien have passed, with a good many others."

Then I knew that he wanted to go, that his mind was made up to a certain extent, and that gave me a shock; for if he once set off, Heaven only knew when his marriage would take place; the thought of Marie-Rose troubled me.

"Very likely," I said; "but you must think of the old people, Jean. What would your mother, good old Margredel, say, if you abandoned her at such a time?"

"My mother is a good Frenchwoman," he answered. "We have talked it over, brigadier; she consents."

My arms dropped at my sides; I did not know what to reply; and only at the end of a minute I managed to say:

"And Marie-Rose! You do not think of Marie-Rose! Yet you are betrothed. She is your wife in the eyes of God!"

"Marie-Rose consents also," he said. "We only want your consent now; say yes; all will be settled. The last time I was here, while you were down stairs smoking your pipe, I told Marie-Rose all about it. I said to her that a forest guard without a situation, an old soldier like me, ought to be at the front; she understood and consented."

When he told me that, George, it was too much; I cried: "I do. It is not possible!" And, opening the window, I called out:

"Marie-Rose! Marie-Rose! Come here. Jean has arrived."

She was hanging out clothes in the shed, and leaving at once her work, she came up stairs.

"Marie-Rose," I said, "is it true that you have consented to let Jean Merlin go to fight the Germans at Orleans, behind Paris? Is it true? Speak freely."

Then, pale as death, with flashing eyes, she said:

"Yes. It is his duty. He must go. We do not wish to be Prussians, and the others ought not to fight alone to save us. He must be a man. He must defend his country."

She said other things of the same kind that warmed my blood and made me think:

"What a brave girl that is! No, I did not know her before. She is the true descendant of the old Burats. How the old people wake up and speak through the mouths of their children! They want us to defend the earth of the old cemetery where their bones lie buried."

I rose, white as a sheet, with open arms.
"Come to my arms!" I said to them; "come to
my arms! You are right. Yes, it is the duty of
every Frenchman to go and fight. Ah! if I were
only ten years younger, I would go with you,
Jean; we would be two brothers in arms." And
we embraced each other all round.

***

XXIV

I WEPT; I was proud of having so brave and
honest a daughter, whom I had not appreciated
till then; that made me lift up my head again.
The resolution of Jean and Marie-Rose appeared
natural to me.

But, as we heard the grandmother groping her
way from the other room, by leaning against the
wall, I made a sign to them to be silent, and,
when the poor old woman came in, I said:

"Grandmother, here is Jean, whom the chief
inspector is about to send to Nancy; he will be
there for some time."

"Ah!" said she. "There is no danger?"

"No, grandmother, it is a commission for the
forest registers; it has nothing to do with the
war."

"So much the better!" said she. "How many others are in danger! We ought to be very happy to keep out of it!"

Then, sitting down, she began, as usual, to say her prayers.

What more can I tell you, George, about those things that rend my heart when I think about them?

Jean Merlin spent the whole day with us. Marie-Rose cooked as good a dinner as she could in our position; she put on her handsome cap and her blue silk *fichu*, so as to be agreeable to the eyes of the man she loved.

I seem to see her still, sitting at the table near the grandmother, opposite her betrothed, and smiling, as if it were a holiday. I seem to hear Jean talking about the good news from Orleans, about the happy chances of the war, which are not always the same.

Then, after dinner, while the grandmother dozes in her arm-chair, I see the two children sitting beside each other, near the little window, looking at each other, holding each other's hand, and talking in a low voice, sometimes gaily, sometimes sadly, as is the custom with lovers.

As for me, I walked up and down, smoking and thinking of the future. I listened to the hum of talk from the tavern, and, remembering the danger of leaving the country, the penalties established by the Germans against those who wished to join our armies, I seemed to hear the stamping of heavy boots and the rattle of sabres. I went down the stairs, and, half opening the door of the smoky room, I looked in, and then I went up stairs again, a little reassured, saying to myself that I ought not to be afraid, that more difficult lines of the enemy had been crossed, and that energetic men always got well through their business. So passed all that afternoon.

Then, at supper, as the time for his departure drew near, a more terrible sadness and strange, unknown fears seized upon me.

"Go to bed," I said to the grandmother; "the night has come."

But she did not hear me, being a little deaf, and she went on muttering her prayers, and we looked at each other, exchanging our thoughts by signs. At last, however, the poor old woman rose, leaning her two hands on the arms of her chair, and murmuring:

"Good night, my children. Come, Jean, till I kiss you. Distrust the Prussians; they are traitors! Do not run any risks; and may the Lord be with you!"

They kissed each other ; Jean seemed touched ; and when the door was closed, as the church clock was striking eight, and when the little panes were growing dark, he said .

"Marie-Rose, the time has come. The moon is rising ; it is lighting already the path by which I must reach the Donon."

She flung herself into his arms and they held each other clasped in a close embrace for a long time, in silence, for down stairs they were talking and laughing still ; strangers might be watching us, so we had to be prudent.

You do not know, George, and I hope that you never will know, what a father feels at such a moment.

At last they separated. Jean took his stick ; Marie-Rose, pale, but composed, said : "*Adieu, Jean!*" And he, without answering, hurried out, breathing as if something was choking him.

I followed him. We descended the dark little staircase, and on the threshold, where the moon, covered with clouds, cast a feeble ray, we also kissed each other.

"You do not want anything?" I said, for I had put about fifty francs in my pocket.

"No," said he, "I have all that I need."

We held each other's hands as if we could

never let go, and we looked at each other as if we could read each other's hearts.

And, as I felt my lips quiver :

"Come, father," said he, in a trembling voice, "have courage ; we are men !"

Then he strode away. I looked at him vanishing in the darkness, blessing him in my heart. I thought I saw him turn and wave his hat at the corner of the path, by the rock, but I am not sure.

When I went in, Marie-Rose was seated on a chair by the open window, her head buried in her hands, weeping bitterly. The poor child had been courageous up to the last minute, but then her heart had melted into tears.

I said nothing to her, and, leaving the small lamp on the table, I went into my room.

These things happened in November, 1870. But much greater sorrows were to come.

XXV

AFTER that for a few days all was quiet. We heard nothing more from Orleans. From time to time the cannon of the city thundered, and was answered by that of the enemy from Quatre Vents and Werhem ; then all was silent again.

Brigadier Frederick

The weather had turned to rain ; it poured in torrents ; the melting snow floated in blocks down the course of the swollen river. People stayed in-doors, cowering close to the fire ; we thought of the absent, of the war, of the marches and counter-marches. The *gens-d'armes* of Bismark Bohlen continued to make their rounds ; we saw them pass, their cloaks dripping with rain. The silence and the uncertainty overwhelmed one. Marie-Rose came and went without saying anything ; she even put on a smiling aspect when my melancholy grew very great ; but I could see from her pallor what she was suffering.

Sometimes, too, the grandmother, when we least expected it, would begin to talk about Jean, asking for news of him. We would answer her by some insignificant thing, and the short ideas of old age, her weakened memory, prevented her from asking more ; she would be contented with what we could tell her, and murmured, thoughtfully :

" Very good ! very good ! "

And then the cares of life, the daily labour, the care of the cattle and of the household, helped us to keep up.

Poor Calas, having no more work to do with us, had turned smuggler between Phalsbourg and the suburbs, risking his life every day to carry a few pounds of tobacco or other such thing to the glacis; it was rumoured at this time that he had been killed by a German sentinel; Ragot had followed him; we heard nothing more of either of them. They have doubtless been sleeping for a long time in the corner of a wood or in some hole or other; they are very fortunate.

One morning, in the large down-stairs room, when we were alone, Father Ykel said to me:

"Frederick, it is known that your son-in-law, Jean Merlin, has gone to join our army. Take care, the Prussians may give you trouble!"

I was all taken aback, and I answered, after a moment:

"No, Father Ykel! Jean is gone to Dôsenheim on business; he is trying to collect old debts; at this time we need money."

"Pshaw!" said he, "you need not hide the truth from me; I am an old friend of the Burats and you. Merlin has not been here for several days; he has crossed the mountain, and he did right; he is a brave fellow; but there are plenty of traitors about here; you have been denounced, so be on your guard."

This warning startled me, and, thinking that it

would be well to tell his mother, Margredel, and his Uncle Daniel, after breakfast, without saying anything to Marie-Rose, I took my stick and set out for Felsberg.

It had stopped raining. The winter sun was shining over the woods, and this spectacle, after leaving our dark nook, seemed to revive me. As the path at the hill passed near the forest house, showing the old roof in the distance, I was touched by it. All my recollections came back to me, and it occurred to me to go and take a look at the cottage, and to look at the inside by standing on the bench by the wall. It seemed as if it would do me good to see once more the old room, wherein the old people had died and where my children had been born! My heart warmed at the idea and I went swiftly on, till, reaching the little bridge between the two willows, covered with frost, I stood still in horror.

A German forest-guard, his green felt hat, with its cock-feathers, set on one side, his long-stemmed porcelain pipe in his great fair mustaches, and with his arms crossed on the window-sill, was smoking quietly, with a calm expression, happy as in his own house. He was looking smilingly at two chubby, fair-haired children, who were playing before the door, and behind him, in the shadow of the room, was leaning a woman, very fat, with red cheeks, calling, gaily :

"Wilhelm, Karl, come in ; here is your bread and butter !"

All my blood seemed to go through my veins at the sight. How hard it is to see strangers in the old people's house, where one has lived till one's old age, from which one has been chased, from no crime of one's own, only because others are masters and turn one out of doors ! It is terrible !

The guard raising his head suddenly, I was afraid he would see me, so I hid myself. Yes, I hid myself behind the willows, hastening to reach the path farther on, and stooping like a malefactor. I would have been ashamed if that man had seen that the former master had found him in his house, in his room, beside his hearth ; I blushed at the idea ! I hid myself, for he might have laughed at the Alsatian, who had been turned out of doors ; he might have enjoyed himself over it. But from that day hatred, which I had never known before, entered my heart ; I hate those Germans, who peacefully enjoy the fruit of our toil, and consider themselves honest people. I abhor them !

From there I went up through the heath to

Brigadier Frederick

Felsberg, feeling very sad and with hanging head.

The poor village seemed as sad as I, among its heaps of mud and dunghills; not a soul was to be seen in the street, where requisitions of all kinds had passed more than once. And at the old schoolhouse, when I tried to lift the latch, I found the door fastened. I listened; no noise nor murmur of children was to be heard. I looked through the window; the copies were hanging there still by their strings, but the benches were empty.

I called, " Father Daniel!" looking up at the first-floor windows, for the garden gate was also closed. Some moments later another door, that of Margredel's house, built against the gable end, opened; Uncle Daniel, an active little man, with coarse woollen stockings, and a black cotton skull cap on his head, appeared, saying:

"Who is there?" I turned round.

"Ah! it is Brigadier Frederick," said he. "Come in!"

"Then you do not live yonder any more?" said I.

"No, since day before yesterday the school has been closed," he answered, sadly.

And in the lower room of the old cottage, near the little cast-iron stove, where the potatoes were cooking in the pot, sending their steam up to the ceiling, I saw Margredel, sitting on a low stool.

XXVI

MARGREDEL wore her usual open, kindly expression, and even her usual smile.

"Ah!" said she, "we have no longer our pretty up-stairs room for our friends. The Germans are hunting us out of every place; we will not know where to go soon! However, sit down there on the bench, Father Frederick, and, if you like, we will eat some potatoes together."

Her good-humour and her courage in such a wretched place made me still more indignant against those who had plunged us all into misfortune; my consternation kept me from speaking.

"Are Marie-Rose and the grandmother well?" asked Margredel.

"Yes, thank God!" I answered; "but we are very uneasy about Jean. The Prussians know that he has gone; Father Ykel has warned me to be on my guard, and I came to warn you."

"Who cares for the Prussians?" said she, shrugging her shoulders contemptuously. "Ah! they are a bad race! Jean has crossed the moun-

tains long before this; if they had been able to
stop him we would have heard of it by this time;
they would have come to tell us, rubbing their
hands with delight; but he has got over; he is a
fine fellow!"

She laughed with all her toothless mouth.

"Those who have to fight him will not laugh.
He is safe with our volunteers! The guns and
cannon are thundering yonder!"

The poor woman saw the bright side of everything, as usual, and I thought:

"What a blessing it is to have a character like
that; how fortunate!"

Uncle Daniel was walking about the room,
saying:

"It is because of Jean's departure that the
bandits shut up my school. They had nothing to
reproach me with; they gave me no explanations;
they simply shut it up, that is all, and just gave
us time enough to carry away our furniture;
they looked at us crossly, crying, '*Schwindt!
schwindt!*'"*

"Yes," cried Margredel, "they are sly hypo-
crites; they strike you heavy blows without warning. In the morning they smile at you, they sit
by the fire like good apostles, they kiss **your**

---

*Quick! quick!

children with tears in their eyes; and then all at
once they change their tone, they collar you, and
turn you out of doors without mercy. Ah! those
good Germans; we know those honest people
now! But they will not always be so proud.
Wait a bit; Heaven is just! Our own people
will come back; Jean will be with them. You
will see, Father Frederick! We will go back to
the forest house; we will celebrate the wedding
there! That is all I can say. Don't you see, you
must trust in God. Now we are suffering for our
sins. But God will put everything to rights,
when we will have finished expiating our faults.
It cannot be otherwise. He uses the Prussians to
punish us. But their turn will come; we will go
to their country. They will see how agreeable it
is to be invaded, robbed, pillaged. Let them have
a care! Every dog has his day!"

She spoke with so much confidence that it in-
fected me; I said to myself:

"What she says is very possible. Yes, justice
will be done, sooner or later! After all, we may
take Alsace again. Those Germans do not like
each other. We would only have to win one
great battle; the break-up would begin at once.
The Bavarians, the Hessians, the Würtembergers,
the Saxons, the Hanoverians, they would all go

home again. We would have it all our own way!"

But, in the meantime, we were in a very sad position. Margredel said that they had enough rye and potatoes to last till the end of the war, and that, with a few *sous'* worth of salt, would be sufficient for them.

Master Daniel compressed his lips and looked thoughtful.

So, having seen how things were getting along at Felsberg, I took leave of my old friends about eleven o'clock, wishing them all the good things in the world.

I avoided passing by the forest house, and I descended the hill of Graufthal by the forest of fir trees among the rocks, leaning on my stick in the steepest places.

I remember meeting, about two-thirds of my way down, old Roupp, an incorrigible thief, with his faded little blouse, his cotton cravat rolled like a rope round his lean neck, and his hatchet in his hand.

He was chopping away right and left, at everything that suited him; huge branches, small fir trees, everything went into his magnificent fagot, which was lying across the path, and as I called to him:

Brigadier Frederick

"Then you are not afraid of the Prussian guards, Father Roupp!"

He began to laugh, with his chin turned up and his scrap of felt hat on the back of his neck, and wiping his nose on his sleeve.

"Ah! brigadier," said he, merrily, "those people don't risk themselves alone in the forest! Unless they come in regiments, with cannon in front of them and uhlans on every side, and ten against one, they always follow the high roads. They are fellows that have a great respect for their skins. Ha! ha! ha!"

I laughed, too, for he only told the truth. But a terrible surprise awaited me a little farther on, at the descent of the rocks.

When I left the wood and saw the little thatched roofs at the foot of the hill, among the heath, I first saw helmets glittering in the narrow lane in front of Father Ykel's hut, and, looking closer, I perceived a ragged crowd of men and women gathered around them; Ykel, at the door of the inn, was talking; Marie-Rose behind, in front of the dark stable, and the grandmother at her little window, with uplifted hands, as if cursing them.

Brigadier Frederick

XXVII

NATURALLY, I began to run through the brush-wood, knowing that something serious was happening, and descending the passage of the old cloister, to make a short cut, I came out behind the stable, at the moment that some one was leaving it, dragging our two cows, tied by the horns.

It was the station-master of Bockberg, named Toubac, a short, thick-set man, with a black beard, whose two tall, handsome daughters were said to be the servants of the Prussian *hauptmann*,* who had lodged at his house since the beginning of the siege.

When I saw this rascal taking away my cattle, I cried :

"What are you doing, thief? Let my cows alone, or I will break every bone in your body."

Then, at my cries, the sergeant and his squad of men, with drawn bayonets, Ykel, Marie-Rose, and even the grandmother, dragging herself along and leaning against the wall, entered the passage.

Marie-Rose cried out to me :

"Father, they want to take away our cows."

And the grandmother said lamentingly :

"Good Heavens! what will we have to live

on? Those cows are our only possession; they are all that we have left!"

The sergeant, a tall, lean man, with a tight-fitting uniform and with a sword at his side, hearing Ykel say, "Here is the master! the cows belong to him!" turned his head, as if on a pivot, and looked at me over his shoulder; he wore spectacles under his helmet, and had red mustaches and a hooked nose; he looked like an owl, who turns his head without moving his body; a very bad face!

The crowd was blocking up the passage and the sergeant cried:

"Back! Clear the premises, corporal, and if they resist, fire upon them!"

The trampling of the *sabots* in the mud and the cries of the grandmother, weeping and sobbing, made this scene fearful.

"These cows suit me," said the station-master to the sergeant; "I will take them; we can go."

"Do they belong to you?" said I, angrily, and clutching my stick.

"That is no affair of mine," said he, in the tone of a bandit, without heart and without honour. "I have my choice of all the cows in the country to replace those that the rascals from Phalsbourg carried off from me at their last sortie. I choose these. They are Swiss cows. I always liked Swiss cows."

"And who gave you the choice?" I cried. "Who can give you other people's property?"

"The *hauptmann*, my friend, the *hauptmann!*" said he, turning up the brim of his hat with an air of importance.

Then several of the crowd began to laugh, saying, "The *hauptmann* is a generous man; he pays those well who give him pleasure."

My indignation overcame me; and the sergeant having ordered his squad of men to go on, at the moment when the station-master, crying "Hue!" was dragging my poor cows after him by the horns, I was about to fall upon him like a wolf, when Marie-Rose took hold of my hands and whispered to me with a terrified look:

"Father, do not stir, they would kill you. Think of grandmother."

My cheeks were quivering, my teeth clenched, red flames were dancing before my eyes; but the thought of my daughter alone in the world, abandoned at this terrible time, and of the grandmother dying of hunger, gave me the strength to keep down my rage, and I only cried:

"Go, scoundrel! Keep the property you have

stolen from me, but beware of ever meeting me alone in the forest!"

The sergeant and his men pretended not to hear; and he, the wretch, said, laughing:

"These cows, sergeant, are as good as mine; after a long search we ended by finding two fine animals."

They had searched all the villages, visited all the stables, and it was on us that the misfortune fell. Marie-Rose, on seeing the poor beasts raised by us at the forest house, could not restrain her tears, and the grandmother, her hands clasped above her gray head, cried:

"Ah! now—now we are lost! Now this is the last stroke. My God, what have we done to deserve such misery!"

I supported her by the arm, asking her to go in, but she said:

"Frederick, let me look once more at those good creatures. Oh! poor Bellotte! Poor Blanchette! I will never see you again!"

It was a heartrending spectacle, and the people dispersed quickly, turning away their heads, for the sight of such iniquities is the most abominable thing on earth. At last, however, we were obliged to ascend to our wretched little rooms, and think over our desolation; we had to think how we should live, now that all our resources were taken away. You know, George, what a cow is worth to a peasant; with a cow in the stable one has butter, milk, cheese, all the necessaries of life; to possess a cow is to be in easy circumstances, two are almost wealth. Up to the present time we could sell the produce and make a few *sous* in that way; now we would have to buy everything at this time of dearth, while the enemy fattened on our poverty.

Ah! what a terrible time it was! Those who come after us will have no idea of it.

XXVIII

ALL that we had left were five or six hundred weight of hay and potatoes. Ykel, who sympathized with all our griefs, said to me the same day :

"Look here, brigadier; what I predicted has come to pass. The Germans hate you, because you refused to serve under them, and because your son-in-law has gone to join the republicans. If they could drive you away, or even kill you, they would do it; but they want still to give themselves airs of justice and highmindedness; for that reason they will strip you of everything to force you to leave the country, as they say 'of your own free will!' Take my advice, get rid of your fodder as quickly as possible, for one of these fine mornings they will come to requisition it, saying that those who have no cows have no need of fodder. And, above all, do not say that I gave this advice!"

I knew that he was right; the next day my hayloft was empty; Gaspard, Hulot, Diederick, Jean Adam, big Starck, all the neighbours came that evening and carried off our provision of hay by bundles, and in this way I had a few francs in reserve. Starck even gave up to me one of his goats, which was of the greatest use to us; at least the grandmother had a little milk, morning and evening, that prolonged her life; but after so many shocks the poor old woman was terribly weakened, she trembled like a leaf, and no longer left her bed, dreaming always, murmuring prayers, talking of Burat, her husband; of Grandfather Duchêne, of all the old people that returned to her memory. Marie-Rose spun beside her, and sat up till late at night, listening to her laboured breathing and her complaints.

I sat alone in the side room, near the little windows, almost blocked with snow, my legs crossed, my unlighted pipe between my teeth, thinking of all the acts of injustice, of all the thefts, of those abominations that took place every day ; I began to lose confidence in the Almighty ! Yes, it is a sad thing to think of, but by dint of suffering I said to myself that among men many resemble the sheep, the geese, and the turkeys, destined to feed the wolves, the foxes and the hawks, who feast themselves at their expense. And I pushed my indignation so far as to say to myself that our holy religion had been invented by malicious people to console fools for being preyed upon by others. You see, George, to what excesses injustice drives us. But the worst of all was, that there was bad news from the interior. A party of Germans came from Wechem to confiscate my hay and found the loft empty ; they were indignant at it ; they asked me what had become of the fodder, and I told them that the station-master's cows had eaten it. My goat happened fortunately to be among those of Starck, or the *bandits* would certainly have carried it off with them.

This troop of brawlers, then going into the inn, related how the republicans had been beaten ; that they had left thousands of corpses on the field of battle ; that they had been repulsed from Orleans, and that they were still pursuing them ; they laughed and boasted among themselves. We did not believe one quarter of what they said, but their good-humoured air and their insolence in speaking of our generals, forced us to think that it was not all a lie.

As to Jean, no letters, no news! What had become of him? This question, which I often asked myself, troubled me. I was careful not to speak of it to Marie-Rose; but I saw by her pallor that the same thought followed her everywhere.

It was now December. For some time the cannon of Phalsbourg had been silenced, it was said that at night flames had been seen to rise suddenly from the ramparts; we wondered what it could be. We have since learned that they were burning the powder and breaking up the artillery material, and they were spiking the cannon, for the provisions were running out and they were about to be forced to open the gates.

This misfortune happened on the thirteenth of December, after six bombardments and a hundred and twenty days of siege. Half the city was in ruins; at the bombardment of the fourteenth of August alone eight thousand five hundred shells had laid whole streets in ruins; and the poor fellows picked up hastily in the suburbs at the time of the terrible heat and sent into the city, with nothing but the blouses on their backs and their shoes on their feet, after having passed that fearful winter on the ramparts, were carried off again as prisoners of war, some to Rastadt, others to Prussia, through the snow. On hearing this news the consternation became universal. As long as the cannon of Phalsbourg thundered we had kept up our hopes. We said from time to time, "France still speaks!" And that made us lift up our heads again; but then the silence told us that the Germans were really our masters, and that we must make ourselves small so as not to draw down their anger upon us.

From that day, George, our sadness knew no bounds. To add to our misfortune, the grandmother grew much worse. One morning when I entered her room, Marie-Rose said to me in a low voice:

"Father, grandmother is very sick. She does not sleep any more. She seems suffocating! You ought to go for the doctor."

"You are right, my daughter," said I; "perhaps we have waited too long as it is."

And, in spite of the pain of seeing our old fortress in the enemy's hands, I determined to go to Phalsbourg in search of a physician. That day the country was nothing but mud and clouds. I went straight forward, with drooping head, walking on the slope at the edge of the road, my mind a blank, from having thought for so many months of our abasement, and so downcast that I would have given my life for nothing.

On the plateau of Bugelberg, just outside of the forest, seeing before me about three leagues distant the little city looking as if crushed under the gloomy sky, its burned houses, its ruined church, its ramparts levelled with the ground, I stopped for a moment, leaning on my stick and recalling bygone days.

How many times during the past twenty-five years I had gone there on Sundays and holidays with my poor wife, Catherine, and my daughter, either to go to mass, or to see the booths of the fair, or to shake hands with some old comrades, laughing, happy, thinking that everything would continue that way till the end of our days! And all the vanished joys, the old friends, who, in their little gardens at the foot of the glacis, called to us to come to pick currants or to gather a bunch of flowers, seemed to return. How many recollections returned to me! I could not remember them all, and I cried to myself:

"Oh! how distant those things are! Oh! who would ever have believed that this misfortune would come upon us, that we, Frenchmen and Alsatians, should be obliged to bow our necks to the Prussian yoke !"

My sight grew dim, and I set out again on my journey, murmuring in my soul the consolation of all the wretched :

" Bah ! life is short. Soon, Frederick, all will be forgotten. So take courage, you have not much longer to suffer."

I seemed also to hear the trumpet of our joyous soldiers ; but at the gate, a squad of Germans, in big boots, and their sentinel, with bow-legs, his gun on his shoulder, his helmet on the back of his neck, and, walking to and fro in front of the guard-house, recalled to me our position. My old comrade, Thomé, city overseer and collector of the city duties, beckoned to me to come in. We talked over our misfortunes ; and, seeing that I was looking at a company of Prussians crossing the bridge, who, holding themselves erect, were keeping step, he said :

" Do not look at them, Frederick, they are proud when one looks at them ; they think that we are admiring them."

Then I turned away my eyes, and having rested for a few minutes I entered the city.

XXIX

Do I need to describe to you now the desolation of that poor Phalsbourg, formerly so neat, the little houses so well built, the large parade ground, so gay on review day? Must I tell you of the houses fallen over on each other, the gables overturned, the chimneys in the air amid the ruins; and of the taverns filled with Germans, eating, drinking and laughing, while we, with long faces, looking scared, wretched and ragged after all these disasters, saw these intruders enjoying themselves with their big pay taken out of our pockets? No, only at the thought of it, my heart sickens; it is a thousand times worse than all that people relate.

As I reached the corner of the parade ground, opposite the church tower, which was still standing, with its cracked bells and its virgin with uplifted arms, a harsh voice called from the statehouse:

"*Heraus!*" *

It was the sergeant of the station who was ordering his men to go out; the patrolling officer was coming, the others hastened from the guardhouse and formed the ranks; it was noon. I had

* Get out.

halted in consternation before the Café Vacheron.
A crowd of poor people, homeless, without work
and without food, were walking backward and forward, shivering with their hands in their pockets
up to the elbows; and I, knowing from what
Thomé had said that the military hospital and the
college were crowded with the sick, asked myself
if I could find a doctor to visit at Graufthal a
poor old woman at the point of death. I was
overwhelmed with sadness and doubt. I did not
know to whom to address myself or what to do,
when an old friend of the forest house, Jacob
Bause, the first trout fisher of the valley, began to
call behind me :

"Hallo ! it is Father Frederick ? Then you
are still in the land of the living ?"

He shook hands and seemed so glad to see me
that I was touched by it.

"Yes," said I, "we have escaped, thank God.
When one meets people now one almost thinks
that they have been resuscitated, Unfortunately grandmother is very ill and I do not know
where to find a doctor in the midst of this confusion."

He advised me to go to Dr. Simperlin, who
lived on the first floor of the Café Vacheron, saying that he was a good and learned man, and a

true Frenchman, who would not refuse to accompany me, in spite of the length of the road and the work he had in the town, at the time of this extraordinary press of business. So I went up stairs; and Dr. Simperlin, who was just sitting down to dinner, promised to come as soon as he had finished his repast. Then, feeling a little more easy, I went down stairs into the large coffee room, to take a crust of bread and a glass of wine, while waiting for him. The room was filled with *landwehr*; fat citizens in uniform, brewers, architects, farmers, bankers, and hotel-keepers, come to take possession of the country under the command of the Prussian chiefs, who made them march like puppets.

All these people had their pockets full of money, and to forget the unpleasantness of their discipline they ate as many sausages with sauer-kraut, and as much ham and salad with cervelats as our veterans used formerly to drink glasses of brandy. Some drank beer, others champagne or burgundy, each according to their means, of course without offering any to their comrades— that is understood; they all ate with two hands, their mouths open to the ears, and their noses in their plates; and all that I say to you is, that as this muddy, rainy weather prevented us from opening the windows, one had sometimes to go outside in order to breathe.

I seated myself in one corner with my mug of beer, looking at the tobacco smoke curling round the ceiling, and the servants bringing in what was wanted, thinking of the sick grandmother, of the ruins that I had just seen, listening to the Germans, whom I did not understand, for they spoke an entirely different tongue from that of Alsace; and at the other end of the room some Phalsbourgers were talking of an assistance bureau that was being organized at the State House, of a soup kitchen that they wished to establish in the old cavalry barracks, for the poor; of the indemnities promised by the Prussians, and on which they counted but little.

The time passed slowly. I had ended by not listening at all, thinking of my own misery, when a louder, bolder voice drew me from my reflections; I looked: it was Toubac, the station-master of Bockberg, who was interrupting the conversation of the Phalsbourgers, who cried, audaciously thumping the table with his big fist:

"It is all very well for you, city people, to talk now about the miseries of war. You were behind your ramparts, and when the shells came you ran into your casemates. No one could take anything from you. Those whose houses are burned will receive larger indemnities than they are worth ; the old, worm-eaten furniture will be replaced by new, and more than one whose tongue was hanging before the campaign can rub his hands and stick out his stomach, saying : 'The war has made me a solid citizen ; I have paid my debts and I pass for a famous warrior because my cellar was bullet proof. I will devote myself to staying in my country to buy cheap the goods of those who are going away with the money from my indemnities ; I will sacrifice myself to the end as I have done from the beginning.' Yes, that kind of war is agreeable ; behind strong walls all goes well. While we poor peasants, we were obliged to feed the enemies, to give them hay, straw, barley, oats, wheat, and even our cattle, do you hear ?—our last resource. They took my two cows, and now who shall I ask to repay me for them ? "

This was too much. When he said that, the effrontery of the rascal made me so indignant that I could not help calling to him from my place :

" Ah ! wicked scoundrel, do you dare to boast of your sufferings and of your noble conduct during our misfortunes ? Speak of your sacrifices and the good example that your daughters set. Tell those gentlemen how, having searched the country with a squad of Germans, who gave you your choice among all the animals of the mountains and the plain, to replace your wretched beasts, after having stolen, by this means, my two beautiful Swiss cows, you are not yet satisfied. You dare to complain, and to undervalue honest folk who have done their duty ? "

As I spoke, thinking that this rascal was the cause of the grandmother's illness, I grew more and more angry ; I would have restrained myself, but it was too much for me, and all at once, seizing my stick with both hands, I rushed upon him to knock him down.

Fortunately, Fixeri, the baker, who was sitting beside this rascal, seeing my uplifted stick, parried the blow with his chair, saying :

" Father Frederick, what are you thinking about ? "

This had a terrible effect ; all the room was in a commotion and trying to separate us. He, the thief, finding himself behind the others, shook his fist at me and cried :

" Old rascal ! I will make you pay for that ! The Germans would have nothing to do with you. The Oberförster turned you out. You would have liked to have served under them, but they knew you ; they slammed the door in your face.

That annoys you. You insult honest people; but look out, you will hear from me soon."

These astounding lies made me still more furious; it took five or six men to hold me, so as to prevent me from getting at him.

I should have ended by turning everything upside down, if the *landwehr* had not called a party of watchmen who were passing along the road. Then, hearing the butt ends of the muskets as they were grounded at the door, and seeing the helmets in front of the window, I sat down again, and everything calmed down.

The corporal came in; Mme. Vacheron made him take a glass of wine at the bar, and as the noise had ceased, after wiping his mustaches, he went out, making the military salute. But Toubac and I looked at each other with sparkling eyes and quivering lips. He knew, the wretch, that now his shame would be discovered all through the city, and that made him beside himself with rage.

As for me, I thought, "Only manage to be in my way going to Biechelberg; I will pay you off for all that you have done; the poor grandmother will be avenged."

He, doubtless, had the same thoughts, for he looked at me sideways, with his rascally smile. I was very glad when Dr. Simperlin appeared on the threshold of the room, making me a sign to follow him.

I left at once, after having paid for my glass of wine, and we set out for Graufthal.

XXX

You know, George, how much bad weather adds to one's melancholy. It was sleeting, the great ruts full of water were ruffled by the wind. Dr. Simperlin and I walked for a long time in silence, one behind the other, taking care to avoid the puddles in which one could sink up to his knees.

Farther on, after having passed the Biechelberg, on the firmer ground of the forest, I told the doctor about the offers that the Oberförster had made to us, and the refusal of all our guards except Jacob Hepp; of our leaving the forest house, and of our little establishment at Ykel's, in a cold corner of the wretched inn, under the rocks, where the grandmother had not ceased to cough for six weeks.

He listened to me with bent head, and said at the end that it was very hard to leave one's home,

one's fields, one's meadows, and the trees that one
has planted; but that one should never draw back
before one's duty; and that he also was about to
leave the country with his wife and children,
abandoning his practice, the fruit of his labour for
many years, so as not to become one of the herd
of King William.

Talking thus, about three o'clock, we reached
the wretched tavern of Graufthal. We ascended
the little staircase. Marie-Rose had heard us; she
was at the door, and hastened to offer a chair to
Dr. Simperlin.

The doctor looked at the black beams of the
ceiling, the narrow windows, the little stove, and
said :

" It is very small and very dark for people accustomed to the open air."

He was thinking of our pretty house in the
valley, with its large, shining windows, its white
walls. Ah! the times had changed sadly.

At last, having rested for a few minutes, to get
his breath, he said :

" Let us go see the invalid."

We entered the little side room together. The
day was declining; we had to light the lamp, and
the doctor, leaning over the bed, looked at the
poor old woman, saying :

Brigadier Frederick

"Well, grandmother Anne, I was passing by Graufthal, and Father Frederick beckoned me in; he told me that you were not very well."

Then the grandmother, entirely aroused, recognised him and answered:

"Ah! it is you, M. Simperlin. Yes, yes; I have suffered, and I suffer still. God grant it will soon be over!"

She was so yellow, so wrinkled and so thin, that one thought when one looked at her:

"Good heavens, how can our poor lady continue to exist in such a condition!"

And her hair, formerly gray, now white as snow, her hollow cheeks, her eyes glittering, and a forehead all shrivelled with wrinkles, made her, so to speak, unrecognisable.

The doctor questioned her; she answered very well to all his questions. He listened with his ear at her chest, and then at her back, while I held her up. At last he said, smiling:

"Well, well, grandmother, we are not yet in danger. This bad cold will pass away with the winter; only you must keep yourself warm, and not give way to sad thoughts. You will soon return to the forest house; all this cannot last."

"Yes, yes," said she, looking at us. "I hope that all will come right; but I am very old."

Brigadier Frederick

"Bah! when one has kept up like you, is one old? All this has been caused by a draught; you must take care of draughts, Mlle. Marie-Rose. Come, keep up your courage, grandmother."

So said the doctor; the grandmother seemed a little reassured.

We left the room, and outside, when I was questioning him and my daughter was listening, Dr. Simperlin asked me:

"Shall I speak before Mlle. Marie-Rose?"

"Yes," I answered, "for my poor daughter takes care of the invalid, and she ought to know all; if the illness is serious, if we are to lose the last creature who loves us and whom we love— well, it is always best to know it beforehand, than to be struck by the misfortune without having been warned."

"Well," said he, "the poor woman is ill not only because of her old age, but principally because of the grief which is sapping her constitution. She has something preying upon her mind, and it is that which makes her cough. Take care not to grieve her; hide your troubles from her. Always look gay before her. Tell her that you have strong hopes. If she looks at you, smile at her. If she is uneasy, tell her it is nothing.

Let no one come in, for fear they should tell her bad news; that is the best remedy I can give you."

While he spoke, Marie-Rose, who was very much alarmed, was coughing behind her hand, with a little hacking cough; he interrupted himself, and, looking at her, he said :

"Have you coughed like that for any length of time, Mlle. Marie-Rose ?"

"For some time," she answered, flushing.

Then he took her arm and felt her pulse, saying as he did so :

"You must be careful and look after yourself, too ; this place is not healthy. Have you fever at nights ?"

"No, sir."

"Well, so much the better ; but you must take care of yourself ; you must think as little as possible of sad things."

Having said that, he took his hat from my bed and his cane from the corner, and said to me, as we were descending the stairs together :

"You must come to the city to-morrow, and you will find a little bottle at the shop of Reeb, the apothecary ; you must give three drops of it, in a glass of water, morning and evening, to the grandmother ; it is to calm that suffocating feeling ; and look after your daughter, too ; she is very much changed. When I remember Marie-Rose, as fresh and as healthy as she was, six months ago, it makes me uneasy. Take care of her."

"Gracious Heavens!" said I to myself, in despair ; "take care of her! Yes, yes, if I could give her my own existence ; but how take care of people who are overwhelmed by fears, grief, and regrets?"

And, thinking of it, I could have cried like a child. M. Simperlin saw it, and, on the threshold, shaking my hand, he said :

"We, too, are very sick ; is it not so, Father Frederick ? Yes, terribly sick. Our hearts are breaking ; each thought kills us ; but we are men ; we must have courage enough for everybody."

I wanted to accompany him at least to the end of the valley, for the night had come ; but he refused, saying :

"I know the way. Go up stairs, Father Frederick, and be calm before your mother and your daughter ; it is necessary."

He then went away and I returned to our apartments.

Brigadier Frederick

XXXI

Two or three days passed away. I had gone to the town to get the potion that the doctor had ordered from Reeb, the apothecary; the grandmother grew calmer; she coughed less; we talked to her only of peace, tranquility, and the return of Jean Merlin, and the poor woman was slowly recovering; when, one morning, two Prussian *gensd'armes* stopped at the inn; as those people usually passed on without halting, it surprised me, and, a few moments later, Father Ykel's daughter came to tell me to go down stairs, that some one was asking for me.

When I went down, I found those two tall fellows, with jack-boots, standing in the middle of the room; their helmets almost touched the ceiling. They asked me if they were speaking to the person known as Frederick, formerly the brigadier forester of Tömenthal. I answered in the affirmative; and one of them, taking off his big gloves, in order to fumble in his knapsack, gave me a letter, which I read at once.

It was an order from the commander of Phalsbourg to leave the country within twenty-four hours!

You understand, George, what an impression

that made on me; I turned pale and asked what could have drawn upon me so terrible a sentence.

"That is no affair of ours," answered one of the *gens-d'armes*. "Try to obey, or we will have to take other measures."

Thereupon they mounted their horses again and rode off; and Father Ykel, alone with me, seeing me cast down and overwhelmed by such an abomination, not knowing himself what to say, or to think, cried out:

"In the name of Heaven, Frederick, what have you been doing? You are not a man of any importance, and, in our little village, I should have thought they would have forgotten you long ago!"

I made no reply; I remembered nothing; I thought only of the grief of my daughter and of the poor old grandmother when they learned of this new misfortune.

However, at last I remembered my imprudent words at the Café Vacheron, the day of my dispute with Toubac; and Father Ykel at the first word told me that it all came from that; that Toubac had certainly denounced me; that there was only one thing left for me to do, and that was to go at once to the commander and beg him to grant me a little time, in consideration of the grandmother, over eighty years of age, seriously ill, and who would certainly die on the road. He also sent for the schoolmaster, and gave me, as Mayor of the parish, a regular attestation concerning my good qualities, my excellent antecedents, the unhappy position of our family ; in short, he said all the most touching and the truest things that could be said on such an occasion. He also recommended me to go to M. Simperlin, too, and get a certificate of illness, to confirm his attestation, thinking that thus the commander would be touched and would wait till the poor old woman was well enough to travel.

In my trouble, seeing nothing else to do, I set out. Marie-Rose knew nothing of it, nor the grandmother, either ; I had not the courage to announce the blow that was threatening us. To set out alone, to fly far away from those savages, who coolly plunged us into all sorts of miseries, would have been nothing to me ; but the others ! Ah ! I dared not think of it !

Before noon I was at Phalsbourg, in a frightful state of wretchedness ; all the misfortunes that crushed us rose before my eyes.

I saw the doctor, who declared simply in his certificate that the invalid, who was old, weak, and, moreover, entirely without resources, could not stand a journey, even of two hours, without dying.

"There," said he, giving me the paper, "that is the exact truth. I might add that your departure will kill her also, but that would be nothing to the commander; if this does not touch his heart, the rest would be useless also."

I went then to the commander's quarters, which were in the old government house, in the Rue du Collége. The humiliation of addressing supplications to rascals whom I detested was not the least of my sorrows; that I, an old French forester, an old servant of the state, gray-headed and on the point of retiring on a pension, should stoop to implore compassion from enemies as hard-hearted, as proud of their victories, gained by sheer force of numbers, as they were! However, for the grandmother, for the widow of old Burat, I could bear everything.

A tall rogue, in uniform, and with red whiskers, made me wait a long time in the vestibule; they were at breakfast, and only about one o'clock was I allowed to go up stairs. Up there another sentinel stopped me, and then, having received permission to enter a rather large room, opening on the garden of the Arsenal, I knocked at the commander's door, who told me to come in. I saw a large, red-faced man, who was walking to and fro, smoothing down the sleeves of his uniform and puffing out his cheeks in an ill-natured way. I told him humbly of my position, and gave him my certificates, which he did not even take the trouble to read, but flung them on the table.

"That has nothing at all to do with it," said he sharply; "you are described as a dangerous person, a determined enemy of the Germans. You prevented your men from entering our service; your son-in-law has gone to join the bandits of Gambetta. You boasted openly in a restaurant of having refused the offers of the Oberförster of Zornstadt; that is four times more than is necessary to deserve being turned out of doors."

I spoke of the grandmother's condition.

"Well! leave her in her bed," said he; "the order of the *Kreissdirector* is for you alone."

Then, without listening to me any longer, he went into a side room, calling a servant, and closed the door behind him. I went down stairs again, feeling utterly crushed; my last hope was gone; I had no other resource; I had to leave; I had to announce this bad news to my daughter, to the grandmother! I knew what would be the result of it; and, with hanging head, I went through that German doorway, the bridge, the sentinels, without seeing anything. On the glacis, at Bie-chelberg, all along the road through the woods and through the valley, I was as if mad with despair; I talked to myself, I cried out, looking at the trees and raising my hand toward heaven.

"Now the curse is upon us! Now pity, the disgrace of crime, the remorse of conscience are abolished! Nothing is left now but strength. Let them exterminate us, let them cut our throats! Let the rascals strangle the old woman in her bed; let them hang my daughter before the door, and as for me, let them chop me into pieces! That would be better. That would be less barbarous than to tear us from each other's arms; to force the son to abandon his mother on her death-bed!"

And I continued on my road, stumbling along. The forests, the ravines, the rocks seemed to me full of those old brigands, of those Pandoms of whom I had heard tell in my childhood; I thought I heard them singing round their fires, as they shared the plunder; all the old miseries of the time before the great revolution came back to me. The distant trumpet of the Prussians in the city that sounded its three wild notes to the echoes, seemed to me to arouse those old villains who had been reduced to dust centuries before.

XXXII

ALL at once the sight of the cottages of Graufthal aroused me from my dreams; I shivered at the thought that the moment was come to speak, to tell my daughter and the grandmother that I was banished, driven away from the country. It seemed to me like a sentence of death that I myself was about to pronounce against those whom I loved best in the world. I slackened my steps so as not to arrive too quickly, when, raising my eyes, after having passed the first houses, I saw Marie-Rose waiting in the dark little entry of the inn; my first glance at her told me that she knew all.

" Well, father?" said she in a low voice, as she stood on the threshold.

"Well," I answered, trying to be calm, " I must go. But you two can stay—they have granted you permission to stay."

At the same time I heard the grandmother moaning up stairs in her bed. Katel, that morning, directly after I set out, had gone up stairs to tell my daughter the bad news; the poor old woman had heard all. The news had already spread through the village; the people round us were listening; and, seeing that the blow had

fallen, I told all who wished to hear how the
Prussian commander had received me. The
crowd of neighbours listened to me without a
word ; all were afraid of sharing my fate. The
grandmother had heard my voice, and she called
me :

"Frederick ! Frederick !"

When I heard her voice, a cold perspiration
broke out on my face. I went up stairs, answering :

"Here I am, grandmother, here I am ! Don't
cry so ! It will not last long. I will come back !
Now they distrust me. They are wrong, grandmother ; but the others are the strongest !"

"Ah !" she cried, "you are going away, Frederick—you are going away like poor Jean. I
knew that he had gone away to fight. I knew
all. I will never see either of you again."

"Why not, grandmother, why not ? In a few
weeks I will be allowed to come back, and Jean
will come back, too, after the war !"

"I will never see you again !" she cried.

And her sobs grew louder. The people, curious, and even cruel in their curiosity, had come
up stairs one after another ; our three little rooms
were filled with them ; they held their breath, they
had left their *sabots* at the foot of the stairs ; they

wanted to see and hear everything; but then, seeing the poor old woman in the shadow of her great gray curtains, sobbing and holding out her arms to me, almost all hastened to go down stairs again and to return to their homes. No one was left but big Starck, Father Ykel, and his daughter, Katel.

"Grandmother Anne," said Father Ykel, "don't get such ideas into your head. Frederick is right. You must be reasonable. When peace is declared all will be right again. You are eighty-three years old and I am nearly seventy. What does that matter? I hope to see again Jean, Father Frederick, and all those who are gone."

"Ah!" said she, "I have suffered too much; now it is all over!"

And till night she did nothing but cry. Marie-Rose, always courageous, opened the cupboards and packed up my bundle, for I had no time to lose; the next day I must be on my road. She took out my clothes and my best shirts and put them on the table, asking me, in a low voice, while the grandmother continued to cry:

"You will take this, father? And that?"

I answered:

"Do as you think best, my daughter. I have no sense left to think of anything with. Only put my uniform in the bundle—that is the principal thing."

Ykel, knowing that we were pressed for time, told us not to worry about the supper, that we should sup with them. We accepted.

That evening, George, we spoke little at table. Katel was up stairs with the grandmother. And when night came, as my bundle was packed, we went to bed early.

You may readily believe that I slept but little. The moans of the grandmother, and then my reflections, the uncertainty as to my destination, the small amount of money that I could take with me, for I had to leave enough to live on at home—all these things kept me awake in spite of my fatigue and the grief that was weighing me down. And all through that long night I asked myself where I should go, what I should do, what road I should take, to whom I should address myself in order to make my living? Turning these ideas over a hundred times in my head, I at last remembered my former chief of the guards, M. d'Arence, one of the best men I had ever known, who had always liked me, and even protected me during the time that I was under his orders as a simple guard many years before; I remembered that people said that he had retired to Saint Dié, and I hoped, if I had the good luck to find him yet alive, that he would receive me well and would help me a little in my misfortune. This idea occurred to me towards morning; I thought it a good one, and I fell asleep for an hour or two. But at daybreak I was up. The terrible moment was approaching; I was scarcely out of bed, the grandmother heard me and called to me. Marie-Rose was also up; she had prepared our farewell breakfast; Ykel had sent up a bottle of wine.

Having dressed myself, I went into the grandmother's room, trying to keep up my spirits, but knowing that I would never see her again.

She seemed calmer, and, calling me to her, she threw her arms round my neck, saying:

"My son, for you have been my son—a good son to me—my son Frederick, I bless you! I wish you all the happiness that you deserve. Ah! wishes are not worth much, nor the blessings of poor people either. Without that, dear Frederick, you would not have been so unhappy."

She wept, and I could not restrain my tears. Marie-Rose, standing at the foot of the bed, sobbed silently.

And as the grandmother still held me, I said:

"See here, grandmother, your benediction and your kind words do me as much good as if you could give me all the riches of the world ; it is my consolation to think that I will see you soon again."

" Perhaps we will meet again in heaven," said she ; " but here on this earth I must say farewell. Farewell, Frederick, farewell."

She held me tightly embraced, kissing me with her trembling lips ; and then, having released me and turned away her head, she held my hand for a minute, and, beginning to sob again, she repeated, in a low voice : " Farewell !"

I left the room ; my strength failed me. In the side room I took a glass of wine and I put a piece of bread in my pocket ; Marie-Rose was with me ; I beckoned her to come down stairs softly, so that the grandmother should not hear our sobs at the moment of parting.

We went silently down stairs into the large lower room, where Father Ykel awaited us with some other friends ; Starck, who had helped us to move from the forest house, Hulot, and some other good people.

We bade each other farewell ; then in the entry I kissed Marie-Rose, as an unhappy father kisses his child, and in that kiss I wished her everything that a man can wish to the being whom he loves better than his life, and whom he esteems as one esteems virtue, courage, and goodness. And then, with my bundle slung on the end of a stick, I went away without turning my head.

XXXIII

THE path of exile is long, George, and the first steps that one takes are painful. He who said that we do not drag with us our country fastened to the soles of our shoes, was learned in human suffering.

And when you leave behind you your child; when you seem to hear as you walk along the grandmother's voice saying farewell; when from the top of the mountain that sheltered you from the wind and covered you with its shadow, at the last turn of the path, before the descent, you turn and look at your valley, your cottage, your orchard, thinking, "You will never see them more!" then, George, it seems as if the earth holds you back, as if the trees were extending their arms towards you, as if the child was weeping in the distance, as if the grandmother was calling you back in the name of God!

Yes, I felt all that on the hill of Berlingen, and I shudder yet when I think of it. And to think that worms like us dare to inflict such sufferings on their fellow-creatures! May the Almighty have mercy upon them, for the hour of justice will surely come.

I tore myself away and continued my journey. I went away; I descended the hill with bent back, and the dear country gradually vanished into the distance. Oh! how I suffered, and how many distant thoughts came back to me! The forests, the firs, the old saw-mills passed away.

I was approaching Schönbourg, and I began to descend the second hill, lost in my reveries and my despair, when all at once a man with his gun slung over his shoulder emerged from the forest about a hundred yards in front of me, looking towards me. This sight awoke me from my sad thoughts; I raised my eyes. It was Hepp, the old brigadier, whom the Prussians had won over, and who was the only man among us that had entered their service.

"Hillo!" said he, in amazement, "it is you, Father Frederick!"

"Yes," I answered, "it is I."

"But where are you going so early in the morning with your bundle on your shoulder?"

"I am going where God wills. The Germans

have turned me out. I am going to earn my living elsewhere."

He turned very pale. I had stopped for a minute to breathe.

"How!" said he, "they are turning you out of doors at your age—you, an old forester, an honest man, who never did harm to any one?"

"Yes; they do not want me in this country any longer. They have given me twenty-four hours in which to quit old Alsace, and I am on my way."

"And Marie-Rose and the grandmother?"

"They are at Graufthal, at Ykel's. The grandmother is dying. The others will bury her."

Hepp, with drooping head and eyes cast down, lifted up his hands, saying : "What a pity! what a pity!"

I made no reply, and wiped my face, which was covered with perspiration. After a moment's pause, without looking at me, he said :

"Ah! if I had been alone with my wife! But I have six children. I am their father. I could not let them die of hunger. You had a little money laid aside. I had not a *sou*."

Then, seeing this man with a good situation—for he was a German brigadier forester—seeing this man making excuses to a poor, wretched exile

like me, I did not know any more than he did
what to answer, and I said :

"That is the way of the world. Every one
has his burden to bear. Well! well! good-bye till
I see you again."

He wanted to shake hands with me, but I
looked another way, and continued my journey,
thinking :

"That man, Frederick, is even more unhappy
than you; his grief is terrible; he has sold his
conscience to the Prussians for a piece of black
bread; at least you can look every one in the face;
you can say, in spite of your misery, 'I am an
honest man,' and he does not dare to look at an
old comrade ; he blushes, he hangs his head. The
others have profited by the fact of his having six
children to buy him."

And, thinking of that, I grew a little more
courageous, knowing that I had done well, in spite
of everything, and that in Hepp's place I would
have hanged myself long ago in some corner of
the wood. That comforted me a little. What
would you have? One is always glad to have
done the best thing, even when one had nothing
to choose between but the greatest of misfortunes.

Then those thoughts vanished, too ; others took
their place. I must tell you that in all the villages,

and even in the smallest hamlets I passed through, the poor people, seeing me travelling at my age, with my bundle slung over my shoulder, received me kindly; they knew that I was one of those who were being sent away from the country because they loved France; the women standing before their doors with their children in their arms said to me, with emotion, "God guide you!"

In the little taverns, where I halted from time to time to recruit my strength, at Lutzelbourg, at Dabo, at Viche, they would not receive any money from me. As soon as I had said, "I am an old brigadier forester; the Germans have exiled me because I would not enter their service," I had the respect of everybody.

Naturally, also, I did not accept the kind offers they made me; I paid my way, for at this time of forced requisitions no one had anything too much.

The whole country sympathized with the republic, and the nearer I got towards the Vosges the more they spoke of Garibaldi, of Gambetta, of Chanzy, of Faidherbe; but also the requisitions were larger and the villages overrun with *landwehr*.

At Schirmeck, where I arrived the same day, about eight o'clock in the evening, I saw, on entering the inn, a *Feldwebel*, a schoolmaster, and a commissioner, who were drinking and smoking among a quantity of their people, who were seated at tables like themselves.

They all turned round and stared at me, while I asked a lodging for the night.

The commissioner ordered me to show him my papers; he examined them minutely, the signatures and the stamps; then he said to me :

"You are all right at present, but by daybreak to-morrow you must be on your way."

After that the innkeeper ventured to serve me with food and drink; and, as the inn was filled with the German officials, they took me to the barn, where I fell asleep on a heap of straw. It was freezing outside, but the barn was near the stable; it was warm there; I slept well because of my fatigue. Slumber, George, is the consolation òf the wretched; if I had to speak of the goodness of God, I would say that every day He calls us to Him for a few hours to make us forget our misfortunes.

XXXIV

THE next day a sort of calm had replaced my dejection; I went away more resolute, hastening across the plain to reach Rothau. I began to think of Jean Merlin. Perhaps he had followed the same route as I, for it was the shortest. How glad I would be if I could hear some news of him on my way, to send to Marie-Rose and the grand-mother; what a consolation it would be in our misfortune! But I must not hope for it, so many others during the last three months had climbed from Rothau to Provenchères, French and Germans, strangers whom no one could have remembered.

Nevertheless, I thought of it. And as I walked swiftly along I admired the beautiful forests of this mountainous country, the immense fir trees that bordered the road and recalled to me those of Falberg, near Saverne. The sight of them touched me; it was like old comrades who escort you for several hours on your journey before saying a last farewell.

At last the rapid motion, the fresh, bracing air of the mountains, the kind welcome from the good people, the hope of finding M. d'Arence, my old chief of the guard, and, above all, the wish not to let myself be discouraged, when my poor daughter and the grandmother still had need of me, all that revived me, and I said to myself at each step I took:

"Courage, Frederick! The French are not yet all dead; perhaps after a while the happy days

will return. Those who despair are lost ; the poor
little birds that the winter drives away from their
nests and who are obliged to go far away to seek
the seeds and the insects upon which they live
suffer also ; but the spring brings them back
again. That ought to be an example to you.
Another effort, and you will reach the top ; from
Provenchères you will only have to go down
hill."

Thus encouraging myself climbing on and persevering, as weary as I was, I reached Provenchères
about the middle of the day, and made a short
halt. I drank a glass of good wine at the inn of
the Two Keys, and there I learned that M. d'Arence
was still at St. Dié, the inspector of the woods
and waters, and that he had even commanded the
national guard during the late events. This news
gave me great pleasure ; I left there full of hope ;
and that evening having reached St. Marguerite,
at the bottom of the valley, I had only to follow
the highway till I reached the city, where I arrived
so fatigued that I could scarcely stand.

I halted at the first little tavern in the Rue du
Faubourg St. Martin, and I was fortunate enough
to get a bed there, in which I slept still better
than in my barn at Schirmeck. The Prussian
trumpet awoke me early in the morning ; one of

their regiments was occupying the city; the
colonel was quartered in the episcopal palace, the
other officers and the soldiers were lodged with
the inhabitants; and the requisitions of hay, straw,
meat, flour, brandy, tobacco, etc., were going on
as briskly as at other places. I took a clean shirt
out of my bundle, and put on my uniform, remembering that M. d'Arence had always paid great
attention to the appearance of his men. Character does not change : one is at fifty years of age
exactly as one was at twenty. Then I went down
into the inn parlour, and inquired for the house of
the inspector of the forest. A good old woman,
Mother Ory, who kept the inn, told me that he
lived at the corner of the large bridge, to the left,
as you went towards the railway station. I went
there at once.

It was a clear cold day; the principal street,
which runs from the railway station to the cathe-
dral, was white with snow, and the mountains
round the valley also. Some German soldiers, in
their earth-coloured overcoats and flat caps, were
taking away at a distance, before the mayor's
office, a cartload of provisions; two or three servant maids were filling their buckets at the pretty
fountain of La Muerthe. There was nothing else
to see, for all the people kept in doors.

Brigadier Frederick

Having reached the house of the inspector, and after having paused for a moment to reflect, I was going in, when a tall, handsome man in hussar pantaloons, a tight-fitting braided overcoat, a green cap with silver lace, set a little on one side, began to descend the stair-case. It was M. d'Arence, as erect as ever, with his beard as brown and his colour as fresh as it was at thirty years of age. I recognised him at once. Except for his gray head, he was not changed at all; but he did not recognise me at first; and it was only when I reminded him of this old guard, Frederick, that he cried:

"What, is it you, my poor Frederick? Decidedly we are no longer young."

No, I was no longer young, and these last few months had aged me still more, I know. However, he was very glad to see me all the same.

"Let us go up stairs," he said; "we can talk more at our ease."

So we went up stairs. He took me into a large dark office, the blinds of which were closed, then into his private room, where a good fire was sparkling in a large porcelain stove; and, having told me to take a chair, we talked for a long time about our country. I told him of all our wretchedness since the arrival of the Germans; he listened to me with compressed lips, his elbow on the edge of the desk, and he finally said :

"Yes, it is terrible ! So many honest people sacrificed to the selfishness of a few wretches! We are expiating our faults terribly ; but the Germans' turn will come. In the meantime, that is not the question ; you must be in straitened circumstances ; you are doubtless at the end of your funds ?"

Of course I told him the truth ; I said that I had to leave enough to live on at home, and that I was trying to get work.

Then he quietly opened a drawer, saying that I, like the other brigadiers of Alsace, had a right to my quarter's pay, that he would advance it to me, and that I could repay him later.

I need not tell you my satisfaction at receiving this money at a time when I needed it so much ; it touched me so that my eyes filled with tears and I did not know how to thank him.

He saw by my face what I thought, and, as I tried to utter a few words of thanks, he said :

"All right, all right, Frederick. Don't let us speak of that. You are an honest man, a servant of the state. I am glad to be able to help you."

But what pleased me most of all was that, when I was about to go, he asked me if several of our guards had not joined the army of the Vosges.

Then I instantly thought of Jean; I thought that perhaps he had news of him. In spite of that, I first cited big Kern and Donadieu, and then only Jean Merlin, who had left last, and who had doubtless followed the same road as I had done, by Schirmeck and Rothau.

"A big, solid fellow," said he, "with brown mustaches; formerly in the cavalry, was he not?"

"Yes, sir," I answered, in great excitement; "that is my son-in-law."

"Well," said he, "that honest fellow passed this way; I gave him the means and the necessary indications to reach Tours. If you are uneasy about him, you may be comforted; he is all right; he is at his post."

We had then reached the foot of the stairs; at the door M. d'Arence shook hands with me; then he went away, crossing the bridge, and I went towards the railway station, feeling happier than I can tell you.

XXXV

I ANTICIPATED Marie-Rose's joy, and I seemed to hear the poor grandmother thank God when she heard the good news; it seemed to me that our greatest misfortune had passed away, that the sun was beginning to shine through the clouds for us. I walked along with my head full of happy thoughts; and when I entered the parlour of the Golden Lion, Mother Ory looked at me, saying :

"Ah! my good man, you have had some good luck befall you."

"Yes," I answered, laughing, "I am not the same man I was this morning and yesterday. Great misfortunes don't always stick to one person all the time!"

And I told her what had occurred. She looked at me good-humouredly; but when I asked her to give me some paper, so that I could write all the good news to Graufthal, she said, clasping her hands :

"What are you thinking about? To write that your son-in-law is with the army, that he received aid from M. d'Arence to speed him on his way! Why, M. d'Arence would be arrested tomorrow, and you, too, and your daughter! Don't

you know that the Germans open all the letters;
that it is their best means of spying, and that they
seek every opportunity to levy new taxes on the
city ? For such a letter they would require still
more requisitions. Beware of such fearful im-
prudence."

Then, seeing the justice of her remarks, I suddenly lost all my gaiety ; I had scarcely spirit
enough left to write to Marie-Rose that I had
arrived safe and well and that I had received some
help from my former chief. I thought at every
word that I had said too much ; I was afraid that
a dot, a comma, would serve as a pretext to the
scoundrels to intercept my letter and to drive me
farther away.

Ah ! how sad it was not to be able to send
even a word of hope to those one loves—above
all, at such a cruel moment ! And how barbarous
they must have been to charge against the father
as a crime the consoling words that he sent to his
child, the good news that a son sends to his dying
mother ! But that is what we have seen.

Only the letters announcing the death of one's
relatives, or some new disaster to our country, arrived ; or else lies—news of victories invented by
the enemy, and that was followed the next day by
the announcement of a defeat.

Brigadier Frederick

From that day, not daring to write what I knew, and receiving no news from home, I lived a melancholy life.

Imagine, George, a man of my age, alone among strangers, in a little room at an inn, looking for hours together at the snow whirling against the window-panes, listening to the noises outside, a passing cart, a company of Prussians who were going their rounds, the barking of a dog, people quarrelling; without any amusement but his meditations and his recollections.

"What are they about yonder? Does the grandmother still live? And, Marie-Rose—what has become of her? And Jean, and all the others?" Always this weight on my heart!

"No letters have come; so much the better. If anything had happened, Marie-Rose would have written. She does not write; so much the worse. Perhaps she, too, is ill!"

And so it went on from morning till night. Sometimes, when I heard the hum of voices down stairs in the parlour, I would go down, to hear the news of the war. Hope, that great lie which lasts all one's life, is so rooted in our souls that we cling to it till the end.

So I went down stairs, and there, around the tables, by the stove, were all kinds of people—

merchants, peasants, wagoners—talking of fights in the north, the east ; of pillages, of military executions, of fires, of forced contributions, of hostages, and I know not what all !

Paris was still defending herself ; but near the Loire our young troops had been forced to fall back ; the Germans were too many for them ! They were arriving by all the railroads ; and then our arms and ammunition were giving out. This young army, assembled in haste, without a head, without discipline, without arms, without provisions, was forced to keep up against this terrible war, and the fearful weight of numbers could not fail to crush it after a while.

That is what the Swiss and Belgian newspapers said, that the travellers sometimes left behind them.

The bombardment of Belfort continued. The weather was fearful ; snow and hard frosts followed each other in quick succession. One could almost say that the Almighty was against us.

For my part, George, I must confess that, after so many misfortunes, I was discouraged ; the least rumour made me uneasy ; I was always afraid of hearing of fresh disasters ; and sometimes, too, my indignation made me wish to go, in spite of my old legs, and get myself killed, no matter where, so as to be done with it.

Ennui and discouragement had got the upper hand of me, when I received a letter from my daughter.

The grandmother was dead! Marie-Rose was coming to join me at St. Dié. She told me to hire a small apartment, as she was going to bring a little furniture, some linen, and some bedding, and that she was going to sell the rest at Graufthal before her departure.

She said also that Starck had offered to bring her on his cart, through Sarrebourg, Lorquin, Raon l'Étape; that the journey would probably last fully three days, but that we would meet again at the end of the week.

So the poor grandmother had ceased to suffer; she lay beside her daughter, Catherine, and Father Burat, whom I had loved so much! I said to myself that they were all luckier than I; that they slept among their ancestors, in the shadow of our mountains.

The thought of seeing my daughter once more did me good. I said to myself that we would be no longer alone; that we could live without much expense till the end of the invasion; and then, when Jean returned, when he had found a situation, we would build up our nest again in some forest; that I would have my pension, and that, in spite of all our misfortunes, I would end my days in peace and quietness, among my grand-children.

That appeared very natural to me. I repeated to myself that God is good, and that all would soon be in order again.

Marie-Rose arrived on the fifth of January, 1871.

XXXVI

I HAD rented, for twelve francs a month, two small rooms and a kitchen on the second floor of the house next door to the Golden Lion; it belonged to M. Michel, a gardener, a very good man, who afterward rendered us great services.

It was very cold that day. Marie-Rose had written that she was coming, but without saying whether in the morning or the evening; so I was obliged to wait.

About noon Starck's cart appeared at the end of the street, covered with furniture and bedding.

Marie-Rose was on the vehicle, wrapped in a large cape of her mother's; the tall coalman was walking in front, holding his horses by the bridle.

I went down stairs and ran to meet them. I embraced Starck, who had stopped, then my daughter, saying to her, in a whisper :

" I have heard news of Jean. He passed through St. Dié. M. d'Arence gave him the means to cross the Prussian lines and join the Army of the Loire."

She did not answer, but as I spoke, I felt her bosom heave and her arms tighten round me with extraordinary strength.

They went on again ; a hundred yards farther we were before our lodgings. Starck took his horses to the stable of the Golden Lion. Marie-Rose went into the large parlour of the inn, and good Mother Ory made her take at once a cup of broth, to warm her, for she was very cold.

That same day Starck and I took up the furniture. At four o'clock all was ready. We made a fire in the stove. Marie-Rose was so worn out that we had almost to carry her up stairs.

I had noticed when I first saw her her extreme pallor and sparkling eyes ; it astonished me ; but I attributed the change to the long watches, the grief, the anxiety, and, above all, to the fatigue of a three days' journey in an open wagon, and in such terribly cold weather. Was it not natural after such suffering ? I knew her to be strong ;

since her childhood she had never been ill; I said to myself that she would get over that in time, and that with a little care and perfect rest she would soon regain her rosy cheeks.

Once up stairs, in front of the sparkling little fire, seeing the neat room, the old wardrobe at the back, the old pictures from the forest house hung on the wall, and our old clock ticking away in the right-hand corner behind the door, Marie-Rose seemed satisfied, and said to me :

" We will be very comfortable here, father; we will keep quiet, and the Germans will not drive us farther away. If only Jean comes back soon, we will live in peace."

Her voice was hoarse. She also wanted to see the kitchen, which opened on the court ; the day-light coming from over the roofs made this place rather dark ; but she thought everything was very nice.

As we had not any provisions yet, I sent to the inn for our dinner and two bottles of wine.

Starck would take nothing but the expenses on the road. He said that at this season there was nothing to do in the forest, and that he might as well have come as to have left his horses in the stable ; but he could not refuse a good dinner, and then, too, he liked a good glass of wine.

Brigadier Frederick

Then, at table, Marie-Rose told me all the details of the grandmother's death; how she had expired, after having cried for three days and three nights, murmuring in her dreams: "Burat! Frederick! The Germans! Frederick, do not desert me! Take me with you!" At last the good God took her to Himself, and half Graufthal followed her bier through the snow to Dôsenheim, to bury her with her own people.

In telling her sad tale, Marie-Rose could not restrain her tears, and from time to time she stopped to cough; so I told her that I had heard enough, and that I did not care to know any more.

And when dinner was over, I thanked Starck for the services he had rendered us. I told him that in misfortune we learn to know our true friends, and other just things, which pleased him, because he deserved them. About six o'clock he went away again, in spite of all that I could say to persuade him to remain. I went with him to the end of the street, asking him to thank Father Ykel and his daughter for all that they had done for us, and if he went to Felsberg to tell Mother Margredel how we were getting along, and, above all, to ask her to send us all news of Jean that she might receive. He promised, and we separated.

I went back, feeling very thoughtful; glad to

see my child once more, but uneasy about the terrible cold that kept her from speaking. However, I had no serious fears, as I told you, George. When one has always seen people in good health one knows very well that such little ailments do not signify anything.

There was still seven or eight weeks of winter to pass through. In the month of March the sun is already warm, the spring is coming; in April, sheltered as we were by the great hill of Saint Martin, we would soon see the gardens and the fields grow green again in the shelter of the forest. We had also two large boxes of climbing plants to place on our window-sills, which I pictured to myself beforehand extending over our window-panes, and that would remind us a little of the forest house.

All these things seemed good to me, and, in my emotion at seeing Marie-Rose again, I looked on the bright side of the future; I wanted to live as much to ourselves as we could while waiting for Jean's return, and to worry ourselves about the war as little as possible, although that is very hard to do when the fate of one's fatherland is in question; yes, very hard. I promised myself to tell my daughter nothing but pleasant things, such as tidings of our victories, if we were so fortunate as to gain any, and, above all, to hide from her my uneasiness about Jean, whose long silence often gave me gloomy thoughts.

In the midst of these meditations I returned home. Night had come. Marie-Rose was waiting for me beside the lamp; she threw herself into my arms, murmuring:

"Ah! father, what happiness it is for us to be together once more!"

"Yes, yes, my child," I answered, "and others who are now far away will return also. We must have a little patience still. We have suffered too much and too unjustly for that to last forever. You are not very well now; the journey has fatigued you; but it will be nothing. Go sleep, dear child, and rest yourself."

She went to her room, and I retired to bed, thanking God for having given me back my daughter.

XXXVII

THUS, George, after the loss of my situation and my property, earned by thirty years of labour, economy and faithful services; after the loss of our dear country, of our old parents and our friends, I had still one consolation: my daughter still remained to me, my good, courageous child, who smiled at me in spite of her anxiety, her grief, and her sufferings when she saw me too much cast down.

That is what overwhelms me when I think of it; I always reproach myself for having allowed her to see my grief, and for not having been able to keep down my anger against those who had reduced us to such a condition. It is easy to put a good face on the matter when you have everything you want; in need and in a strange country it is a different thing.

We lived as economically as possible. Marie-Rose looked after our little household, and I often sat for hours before the window, thinking of all that had occurred during the last few months, of the abominable order that had driven me from my country; I suddenly grew indignant, and raised my arms to Heaven, uttering a wild cry.

Marie-Rose was more calm; our humiliation, our misery, and the national disasters hurt her as much and perhaps more than me, but she hid it from me. Only what she could not hide from me was that wretched cold, which gave me much anxiety. Far from improving as I had hoped, it grew worse—it seemed to me to get worse every day. At night, above all, when I heard through the deep silence that dry, hacking cough, that seemed to tear her chest asunder, I sat up in bed and listened, filled with terror.

Sometimes, however, this horrible cold seemed to get better, Marie-Rose would sleep soundly, and then I regained my courage; and thinking of the innumerable misfortunes that were extended over France, the great famine at Paris, the battle-fields covered with corpses, the ambulances crowded with wounded, the conflagrations, the requisitions, the pillages, I said to myself that we had still a little fire to warm us, a little bread to nourish us. And then, so many strange things happened during the wars! Had we not formerly conquered all Europe, which did not prevent us from being vanquished in our turn? Might not the Germans have the same fate? All gamblers end by losing! Those ideas and many others I turned over in my mind; and Marie-Rose said, too:

"All is not over, father; all is not over! I had a dream last night. I saw Jean in a brigadier-forester's costume; we will soon have some good news!"

Alas! good news. Poor child! Yes, yes, you can dream happy dreams; you may see Jean wearing a brigadier's stripes, and smiling at you and giving you his arm to lead you, with a white wreath on your head, to the little chapel at Graufthal, where the priest waits to marry you. All would have happened thus, but there should be fewer rascals on earth, to turn aside the just things established by the Almighty. Whenever I think of that time, George, I seem to feel a hand tearing out my heart. I would like to stop, but as I promised you, I will go on to the end.

One day, when the fire was sparkling in the little stove, when Marie-Rose, very thin and thoughtful, was spinning, and when the old recollections of the forest house, with the beautiful spring, the calm, melancholy autumn, the songs of the blackbirds and thrushes, the murmur of the little river through the reeds, the voice of the old grandmother, that of poor Calas, the joyous barking of Ragot, and the lowing of our two handsome cows under the old willows, came stealing back to my memory; while I was forgetting myself in these things, and while the monotonous hum of the spinning wheel and the ticking of our old clock were filling our little room, all at once cries and songs broke out in the distance.

Marie-Rose listened with amazement; and I, abruptly torn from my pleasant dreams, started like a man who has been roused from sleep. The Germans were rejoicing so, some new calamity had befallen us. That was my first idea, and I was not mistaken.

Soon bands of soldiers crossed the street, arm in arm, crying with all their might :

"Paris has fallen ! Long live the German fatherland !"

I looked at Marie-Rose ; she was as pale as death, and was looking at me also with her great brilliant eyes. We turned our eyes away from each other, so as not to betray the terrible emotion that we felt. She went out into the kitchen, where I heard her crying.

Until dark we heard nothing but new bands, singing and shouting as they passed ; I, with bowed head, heard from time to time my daughter coughing behind the partition of the kitchen, and I gave myself up to despair. About seven o'clock Marie-Rose came in with the lamp. She wanted to set the table.

"It is no use," I said ; "do not put down my plate. I am not hungry."

"Neither am I," said she.

"Well, let us go to bed ; let us try to forget our misery ; let us endeavour to sleep !"

I rose ; we kissed each other, weeping. That night, George, was horrible. In spite of her efforts to stifle the cough I heard Marie-Rose coughing without intermission until morning, so that I could not close my eyes. I made up my mind to go for a doctor; but I did not want to frighten my daughter, and thinking of a means to speak of that to her, towards dawn I fell asleep.

It was eight o'clock when I woke up, and after dressing myself I called Marie-Rose. She did not answer. Then I went into her room, and I saw spots of blood on her pillow; her handkerchief, too, which she had left on the night-table, was all red.

It made me shudder! I returned and sat down in my corner, thinking of what I had just seen.

XXXVIII

It was market day. Marie-Rose had gone to lay in our small stock of provisions; she returned about nine o'clock, so much out of breath that she could scarcely hold her basket. When I saw her come in I recollected the pale faces of those young girls, of whom the poor people of our valley used to say that God was calling them, and who fell asleep quietly at the first snow. This idea struck me, and I was frightened; but then, steadying my voice, I said quite calmly:

Brigadier Frederick

"See here, Marie-Rose, all last night I heard you coughing ; it makes me uneasy."

"Oh ! it is nothing, father," she answered, colouring slightly ; "it is nothing, the fine weather is coming and this cold will pass off."

"Anyhow," I replied, "I will not be easy, as long as a doctor has not told me what it is. I must go at once and get a doctor."

She looked at me, with her hands crossed over the basket, on the edge of the table ; and, guessing perhaps by my anxiety that I had discovered the spots of blood, she murmured :

"Very well, father, to ease your mind."

"Yes," I said, "it is better to do things beforehand ; what is nothing in the beginning may become very dangerous if neglected."

And I went out. Down stairs M. Michel gave me the address of Dr. Carrière, who lived in the Rue de la Mairie. I went to see him. He was a man of about sixty, lean, with black sparkling eyes and a grizzled head, who listened to me very attentively and asked me if I was not the brigadier forester that his friend M. d'Arence had spoken to him about. I answered that I was he, and he accompanied me at once.

Twenty minutes afterward we reached our room. When Marie-Rose came the doctor questioned her for a long time about the beginning of this cold, about her present symptoms, if she had not fever at night with shivering fits and attacks of suffocation.

By his manner of questioning her she was, so to speak, forced to answer him, and the old doctor soon knew that she had been spitting blood for over a month; she confessed it, turning very pale and looking at me as if to ask pardon for having hidden this misfortune from me. Ah! I forgave her heartily, but I was in despair. After that Dr. Carrière wished to examine her; he listened to her breathing and finally said that it was all right, that he would give her a prescription.

But in the next room, when we were alone, he asked me if any of our family had been consumptive; and when I assured him that never, neither in my wife's family nor my own, had we ever had the disease, he said :

" I believe you; your daughter is very beautifully formed; she is a strong and handsome creature; but then she must have had an accident; a fall, or something like that must have put her in this condition. She is probably hiding it from us; I must know it."

So I called Marie-Rose, and the doctor asked her if some weeks before she did not remember having fallen, or else run against something violently, telling her that he was going to write his prescription according to what she would reply, and that her life probably depended upon it.

Then Marie-Rose confessed that the day the Germans came to take away our cows she had tried to hold them back by the rope, and that one of the Prussians had struck her between the shoulders with the hilt of his sword, which had thrown her forward on her hands, and that her mouth had suddenly filled with blood; but that the fear of my anger at hearing of such an outrage had kept her from saying anything to me about it.

All was then clear to me. I could not restrain my tears, looking at my poor child, the victim of so great a misfortune. She withdrew. The doctor wrote his prescription. As we were descending the stairs he said:

"It is very serious. You have only one daughter?"

"She is my only one," I answered.

He was sad and thoughtful.

"We will do our best," he said; "youth has many resources! But do not let her be excited in any way."

As he walked down the street he repeated to

me the advice that M. Simperlin had given me about the grandmother; I made no answer. It seemed to me that the earth was opening under my feet and was crying to me:

"The dead—the dead! Give me my dead!"

How glad I should have been to be the first to go to rest, to close my eyes and to answer:

"Well, here I am. Take me and leave the young! Let them breathe a few days longer. They do not know that life is a terrible misfortune; they will soon learn it, and will go with less regret. You will have them all the same!"

And, continuing to muse in this way, I entered an apothecary's shop near the large bridge and had the prescription made up. I returned to the house. Marie-Rose took two spoonfuls of the medicine morning and evening, as it had been directed. It did her good, I saw it from the first few days; her voice was clearer, her hands less burning; she smiled at me, as if to say:

"You see, father, it was only a cold. Don't worry about it any more."

An infinite sweetness shone in her eyes; she was glad to get well. The hope of seeing Jean once more added to her happiness. Naturally, I encouraged her in her joyous thoughts. I said:

"We will receive news one of these days.

Neighbour such a one also expects to hear from her son; it cannot be long now. The mails were stopped during the war, the letters are lying at the offices. The Germans wanted to discourage us. Now that the armistice is signed we will get our letters."

The satisfaction of learning such good news brightened her countenance.

I did not let her go to the city; I took the basket myself and went to get our provisions; the market women knew me.

"It is the old brigadier," they would say; "whose pretty daughter is sick. They are alone. It is he who comes now."

None of them ever sold me their vegetables at too high a price.

XXXIX

I THOUGHT no longer of the affairs of the country. I only wanted to save my daughter; the rumours of elections, of the National Assembly at Bordeaux, no longer interested me; my only thought was:

"If Marie-Rose only lives!"

So passed the end of January, then came the treaty of peace: we were deserted! And from day to day the neighbours received news from their sons, from their brothers, from their friends, some prisoners in Germany, others in cantonments in the interior ; but for us not a word !

I went to the post-office every morning to see if anything had come for us. One day the postmaster said to me :

"Ah! it is you. The postman has just gone. He has a letter for you."

Then I hastened hopefully home. As I reached the door the postman left the alley and called to me, laughing :

" Hurry up, Father Frederick, you have got what you wanted this time : a letter that comes from the Army of the Loire !"

I went up stairs four steps at a time, with beating heart. What were we about to hear ? What had happened during so many weeks ? Was Jean on the road to come and see us ? Would he arrive the next day—in two, three, or four days ?

Agitated by these thoughts, when I got up stairs my hand sought for the latch without finding it. At last I pushed open the door ; my little room was empty. I called :

" Marie-Rose ! Marie-Rose !"

No answer. I went into the other room ; and my child, my poor child was lying there on the floor, near her bed, white as wax, her great eyes half open, the letter clutched in her hand, a little blood on her lips. I thought her dead, and with a terrible cry I caught her up and laid her on the bed. Then, half wild, calling, crying, I took the letter and read it with one glance.

See, here it is! Read it, George, read it aloud; I know it by heart, but it does not matter, I like to turn the knife in the wound; when it bleeds it hurts less.

"MY DEAR MARIE-ROSE: Adieu! I shall never see you more. A bursting shell has shattered my right leg; the surgeons have had to amputate it. I will not survive the operation long. I had lain too long on the ground. I had lost too much blood. It is all over. I must die! Oh! Marie-Rose, dear Marie-Rose, how I would like to see you again for one instant, one minute; how much good it would do me! All the time I lay wounded in the snow I thought only of you. Do not forget me either; think sometimes of Jean Merlin. Poor Mother Margredel, poor Father Frederick, poor Uncle Daniel! You will tell them. Ah! how happy we would have been without this war!"

The letter stopped here. Underneath, as you see, another hand had written: "Jean Merlin,

Alsatian. Detachment of the 21st Corps. Silly-le-Guillaume, 26th of January, 1871."

I took this all in with one look, and then I continued to call, to cry, and at last I fell into a chair, utterly exhausted, saying to myself that all was lost, my daughter, my son-in-law, my country —all, and that it would be better for me to die, too.

My cries had been heard; some people came up stairs, Father and Mother Michel, I think. Yes, it was they who sent for the doctor. I was like one distracted, without a sign of reason; my ears were singing; it seemed to me that I was asleep and was having a horrible dream.

Long after the voice of Dr. Carrière roused me from my stupor; he said :

"Take him away! Do not let him see this! Take him away!"

Some people took me by the arms; then I grew indignant, and I cried :

"No, sir; I will not be taken away! I want to stay, she is my daughter! Have you children, that you tell them to take me away? I want to save her! I want to defend her!"

"Let him alone," said the doctor, sadly; "let the poor fellow alone. But you must be silent," he said to me; "your cries may kill her."

I fell back in my seat, murmuring :

Brigadier Frederick

"I will not cry out any more, sir; I will say nothing. Only let me stay by her; I will be very quiet."

A few minutes after, Dr. Carrière left the room, making a sign to the others to withdraw.

A great many people followed him, a small number remained. I saw them moving to and fro, arranging the bed and raising the pillows, whispering among themselves. The silence was profound. Time passed. A priest appeared with his assistants; they began to pray in Latin; It was the last offices of the church. The good women, kneeling, uttered the responses.

All disappeared. It was then about five o'clock in the evening. The lamp was lighted. I rose softly and approached the bed.

My daughter, looking as beautiful as an angel, her eyes half open, still breathed; I called her in a whisper: "Marie-Rose! Marie-Rose!" crying bitterly as I spoke.

It seemed every minute as if she was about to look at me and answer, "Father!"

But it was only the light that flickered on her face. She no longer stirred. And from minute to minute, from hour to hour, I listened to her breathing, which was growing gradually shorter and shorter. I looked at her cheeks and her forehead, gradually growing paler. At last, uttering a sigh, she lifted her head, which was slightly drooping, and her blue eyes opened slowly.

A good woman, who was watching with me, took a little mirror from the table and held it to her lips; no cloud dimmed the surface of the glass; Marie-Rose was dead.

I said nothing, I uttered no lamentations, and I followed like a child those who led me into the next room. I sat down in the shadow, my hands on my knees; my courage was broken.

And now it is ended. I have told you all, George.

Need I tell you of the funeral, the coffin, the cemetery? and then of my return to the little room where Marie-Rose and I had lived together; of my despair at finding myself alone, without relations, without a country, without hope, and to say to myself, " You will live thus always—always until the worms eat you ! "

No, I cannot tell you about that; it is too horrible. I have told you enough.

You need only know that I was like a madman, that I had evil ideas which haunted me, thoughts of vengeance.

It was not I, George, who cherished those terrible thoughts; it was the poor creature abandoned by heaven and earth, whose heart had been torn out, bit by bit, and who knew no longer where to lay his head.

I wandered through the streets; the good people pitied me; Mother Ory gave me all my meals. I learned that later. Then I did not think of anything; my evil thoughts did not leave me; I talked of them alone, sitting behind the stove of the inn, my chin on my hands, my elbows on my knees, and my eyes fixed on the floor.

God only knows what hatred I meditated. Mother Ory understood all, and the excellent woman, who wished me well, told M. d'Arence about me.

One morning, when I was alone in the inn parlour, he came to talk things over with me, reminding me that he had always shown himself very considerate towards me, that he had always recommended me as an honest man, a good servant, full of zeal and probity, in whom one could repose perfect trust, and that he hoped it would be that way till the end; that he was sure of it; that a brave, just man, even in the midst of the greatest misfortunes, would show himself the same that he was in prosperity; that duty and honour marched before him; that his greatest consolation and his best was to be able to say to himself: " I am cast down, it is true; but my courage remains to me; my good conscience supports me; my enemies themselves are forced to confess that fate has been unjust to me."

He talked to me in this manner for a long time, pacing up and down the room; and I, who had not shed a tear at my daughter's funeral, I burst out crying.

Then he told me that the time had come to depart; that the sight of the Prussians only embittered my nature; that he would give me a letter of recommendation for one of his intimate friends in Paris; that I would obtain there a situation with a small salary, either on the railway or elsewhere; and that in this way, when my pension was paid to me, I could live in peace, not happy, but far from all that reminded me unceasingly of my misfortunes.

I was ready to do anything that he wished, George, but he wanted nothing but for my own good.

So I set out, and for the last three years I have been one of the superintendents of the Eastern Railway Station.

Brigadier Frederick

XL

When I arrived in the midst of the great confusion after the siege, I had the pain of seeing a terrible thing, the recollection of which adds to my suffering—Frenchmen fighting against Frenchmen. The great city was in flames, and the Prussians outside looked at this sight with a barbarous joy.

"There is no longer any Paris," they said; "no longer any Paris."

The horrible envy that gnawed these people was satisfied.

Yes, I have seen that! I thought that it was all over with us; I shuddered at it. I cried, "The Almighty has determined that France shall descend into the abyss!"

But that, thanks to Heaven, has also passed away. The recollection remains; let us hope that it will never perish.

And that was not all. After these great calamities I was obliged to witness, as I fulfilled the duties of my post, pass, day by day, before my eyes, the great emigration of our brothers of Alsace and Lorraine; men, women, children, old men, by thousands, going to earn their living far from their native land—in Algeria, in America, everywhere.

Brigadier Frederick

Our poor countrymen all recognised me by my face; they said, " He is one of our people."

The sight of them does me good also; it is like a breath from one's native land of good and wholesome air. We shook hands. I pointed them out the hotel where one can live cheaply; I rendered them all the little services that one can render to friends of a day, who will retain a kind remembrance of him who held out his hand to them.

And in the evening, when I went back to my little room under the roof, and thinking about these things, I am still glad at not being quite useless in this world; it is my only consolation, George; sometimes this thought gives me a good night's rest.

Other days, when the weather is gloomy, when it rains, when it is cold, or when I have met in the street the bier of a young girl, with its white wreath, then sad thoughts get the upper hand. I wrap my old cloak around me when my work is over, and I wander aimlessly through the streets, among the people who are all occupied by their own affairs and pay no attention to any one. I walk very far, sometimes to the Arc de Triomphe, sometimes to the Garden of Plants, and I return utterly exhausted. I fall asleep, trying not to think of the happy days of the past, for those remembrances make my heart throb even in a dream, and suddenly I awake, covered with perspiration, and crying :

"All is over. You have no longer a daughter. You are alone in the world."

I am obliged to rise, to light my lamp, and to open the window in order to calm myself a little, to soothe myself and to restore myself to reason.

Sometimes, too, I dream that I am at the forest house with Jean Merlin and Marie-Rose. I see them ; I talk to them ; we are happy. But when I awake—do not let us talk of it ; what is ended cannot return.

Things will go on this way as long as they can. I shall not be buried with the old people, neither with Jean ; nor with my daughter. We will all be scattered. This thought also gives me pain.

I must confess, George, that our brothers of Paris have received us very well ; they have helped us, they have aided us in a hundred ways ; they have done all that they could for us. But after such terrible disasters, they themselves having been so severely tried, the poverty was still very great ; for a long time in the garrets of

Brigadier Frederick

La Villette, of La Chapelle, and of the other suburbs, we suffered from cold and hunger.

To-day the greatest portion of the stream of emigration has passed; almost all the labourers have got work; the women and the old people have found a refuge, and the children are receiving instruction in the public schools.

Others are always coming, the emigation will last as long as the annexation, for Frenchmen cannot bow their heads like the Germans under the Prussians' despotism, and the annexation will last long if we continue to dispute over party questions instead of uniting together in the love of our fatherland.

But do not let us speak of our dissensions; that is too sad.

The only thing that I have still to say to you before ending this sorrowful story is, that in the midst of my misfortunes, I do not accuse the Almighty; no, the Almighty is just; we deserve to suffer. Whence came all our misfortunes? From one man who had taken an oath before God to obey the laws, and who trampled them under his feet, who had those killed who defended them, and transported far away to the islands thousands of his fellow beings whose courage and good sense he feared. Well, this man we ap-

proved of; we voted for him, not once but twenty
times; we took, so to speak, his evil actions upon
ourselves; we threw aside justice and honour; we
thought, "Interest does everything; this man is
shrewd; he has succeeded; we must support
him."

When I remember that I voted for that
wretch, knowing that it was not just, but afraid
of losing my place, when I remember that, I cry,
"Frederick, may God forgive you! You have
lost everything, friends, relatives, country—everything. Confess that you deserved it. You were
not ashamed to support the man who caused
thousands of Frenchmen, as honest as yourself,
also to lose their little all. You voted for
strength against justice; you must bow beneath
the law that you accepted. And, like millions of
others, you, too, gave that man the right to declare war; he did so. He staked you, your country, your family, your possessions, those of all
Frenchmen in the interests of his dynasty, without thinking of anything, without reflecting or
taking any precautions; he lost the game. Pay
and be silent. Do not reproach the Almighty
with your own stupidity and injustice; beat your
breast and bear your iniquity." That is what I
think.

Brigadier Frederick

May others profit by my example; may they always nominate honest people to represent them; may honesty, disinterestedness and patriotism come before anything else; people who are too cunning are often dishonest, and people who are too bold, who do not fear to cry out against the laws, are also capable of upsetting them and of putting their own will in the place of them.

That is the best advice to be given to the French; if they profit by it all will go well, we will regain our frontiers; if they do not profit by it, that which happened to the Alsatians and Lorrainers will happen to them also, province by province; they may repent, but it will be too late.

As to the Germans, they will reap what they have sown. Now they are at the pinnacle of power; they made all Europe tremble, and they are foolish enough to rejoice at it. It is very dangerous to frighten every one; we learned it at our own expense; they will learn it in their turn. Because Bismark has succeeded in his enterprises, they look upon him as a kind of a god; they will not see that this man employed only dishonest means: strategy, lies, espionage, corruption and violence. Nothing is ever firm that is erected on such a foundation.

But to tell all this or nothing to the Germans

would come to the same thing ; they are intoxi-
cated by their victories, and will only awake
when Europe, wearied by their ambition and by
their insolence, will rise to bring them to reason ;
then they will be forced to acknowledge, as we
have acknowledged ourselves, that, if strength
sometimes overwhelms right, justice is eternal.

THE END OF BRIGADIER FREDERICK

THE DEAN'S WATCH

I

THE day before the Christmas of 1832, my friend Wilfrid, his double-bass slung over his shoulder, and I with violin under my arm, were on our way from the Black Forest to Heidelberg. An extraordinary quantity of snow had fallen that season. As far as our eyes could see over the great desert plain before us, not a trace of the route, either of road or path, was to be discovered. The north wind whistled its shrill aria about our ears with a monotonous persistence, and Wilfrid, with wallet flattened against his thin back, his long heron-legs stretched to the utmost, and the visor of his little flat cap pulled down over his nose, strode along before me, humming a gay air from " Ondine." Every now and then he turned his head with a grim smile, and cried:

"Comrade, play me the waltz from ' Robin '— I wish to dance!"

A peal of laughter always followed, and then

3

the brave fellow would push on again with fresh
courage. I toiled on behind in his footsteps, with
the snow up to my knees, and my spirits sinking
lower and lower every moment.

The heights about Heidelberg had begun to
appear on the distant horizon, and we were hoping
to reach the town before nightfall, when we heard
the gallop of a horse behind us. It was about five
o'clock, and great flakes of snow were whirling
about in the gray light. Soon the rider was within
twenty steps. He slackened his pace, examining
us out of one corner of his eye. We also examined him.

Imagine a big man with red beard and hair,
wrapped in a brown cloak, over which was loosely
thrown a pelisse of fox-skins; on his head a
superb cocked-hat; his hands buried in fur gloves
reaching to the elbows. On the croup of his
stout stallion was strapped a well-filled valise.
Evidently he was some burly sheriff, or burgo-
master.

"Hey, my lads!" he cried, drawing one of his
big hands from the muff which hung across his
saddle-bow, and clapping his charger's neck, "we
are going to Heidelberg, I see, to try a little
music."

Wilfrid eyed the traveller askance.

" Is that any affair of yours, sir ? " he answered, gruffly.

" Eh ? yes ; I should have a piece of advice to give you."

" Well, you can keep it till it's asked for," retorted Wilfrid, quickening his pace.

I cast a second glance at our new companion. He looked exactly like a great cat, with ears standing out from his head, his eyelids half closed, and a long, bristling mustache ; altogether he had a sort of purring, paternal air.

" My friend," he began again, this time addressing me, " the best thing you can do is to return whence you came."

" Why, sir ? "

" The famous maestro Prinenti, from Novare, has announced a grand Christmas concert at Heidelberg. Everybody is going to it ; you will not get a single kreutzer."

This was too much for Wilfrid.

" A fig for your maestro, and all the Prinentis in this world ! " he cried, snapping his fingers. " This lad here, with his long curls and blue eyes, and not a hair yet on his chin, is worth an army of your Italian charlatans. Though he never played outside the Black Forest, he can handle a bow with the first musician in Europe, and will draw melody from his violin such as was never heard before in Heidelberg."

"Hear, hear!" cried the stranger.

"It is just as I tell you," said Wilfrid, blowing on his fingers, which were red with the cold.

Then he set out to run, and I followed him as best I might, thinking he wished to make game of the traveller, who kept up with us, however, at a little trot.

In this way we went on in silence for more than half a league. Suddenly the stranger cried out, in a harsh voice :

"Whatever your talents may be, go back to the Black Forest. We have vagabonds enough in Heidelberg already without you. It is good advice I give you—you had best profit by it."

Wilfrid was about to make an angry retort, but the rider had started off at a gallop, and already reached the grand avenue of the elector. At the same moment, a great flock of crows rose from the plain, and seemed to follow him, filling the air with their loud cries.

About seven o'clock in the evening we reached Heidelberg. There, in fact, we found posted on all the walls Prinenti's flaming placards, "Grand Concert, Solo, etc., etc." We wandered about

among the different ale-houses, in which we met
several musicians from the Black Forest, all old
comrades of ours, who immediately engaged us to
play in their band. There were old Bremer, the
violoncellist; his two sons, Ludwig and Carl, capi-
tal second violins; Heinrich Siebel, the clarinet-
player; and big Berthe with her harp. Wilfrid
with his bass-viol, and myself as first violin, made
up the troupe.

It was agreed that we should all go together,
make one purse, and divide after Christmas. Wilfrid had already engaged a room for himself and
me. It was on the sixth story of the little tavern
" Pied-du-Mouton," in the middle of the Holder-
gasse, and was only a garret, though, luckily, it
had a sheet-iron stove, in which we lighted a fire
to dry ourselves.

While we were sitting quietly over the fire,
roasting chestnuts and discussing a pot of wine,
who should come tripping up the stairs and knock
at the door but little Annette, the maid of the inn,
in scarlet petticoat and black-velvet bodice, with
cheeks like roses, and lips as red as cherries!
Next moment she had thrown herself into my
arms with a cry of joy.

We were old friends, the pretty Annette and
I, for we were both from the same village, and, to

say truth, my heart had long been captive to her bright eyes and coquettish airs.

"I saw you go up just now," she said, drawing a stool to my side, "and here I am, come for a minute's talk with you."

With that she began such a string of questions about this one and that—in fact, about every one in our village—that I declare to you it was as much as I could do to answer the half of them. Every little while she would stop and look at me with such a tender air—we would have been there till this time, had not suddenly Mother Gréder Dick screamed from the bottom of the stairs :

"Annette, Annette, are you ever coming?"

"This minute, madame, this minute," cried the poor child, jumping up in a fright. She gave me a little pat on the cheek, and flew to the door. But, just as she was going out, she stopped.

"Ah !" she cried, turning back, "I forgot to tell you. Have you heard——?"

"What ?"

"The death of our pro-recteur Zahn ?"

"Well, what is that to us ?"

"Ah, yes ; but take care, sir, take care—if your papers are not all right ! To-morrow morning, at eight o'clock, they will come to ask for them. They have arrested, oh ! so many people during the last two weeks. The pro-recteur was assassinated yesterday evening, in the library, at the Cloister of Saint-Christophe. Last week the old priest, Ulmet Elias, who lived in the Jews' quarter, was killed in the same way. Only a few days before that they murdered the nurse, Christina Hâas, and Seligmann, the agate-merchant of the Rue Durlach. So, my poor Kasper," she added, with a tender glance, "take good care of yourself, and be sure that your papers are all right."

All the while she was speaking, the cries below continued.

"Annette, O Annette, *will* you come? Oh, the miserable creature, to leave me here all alone!"

And now, too, we could hear the shouts of the guests in the saloon calling for wine, beer, ham, sausages. Annette saw that she must go, and ran down the stairs as quickly as she had come up.

"*Mon Dieu! mon Dieu!*" I heard her soft voice answering her mistress, "what can be the matter, madame, that you should make such an outcry? One would think the house were on fire."

Wilfrid closed the door after her, and came

back to his seat.   We looked at each other with some uneasiness.

"This is strange news," said he at last.   "At any rate, your papers are all in order ?"

"Certainly," I replied, and showed him my pass.

"Good !   There is mine, I had it viséed before we left.   But still, all these murders bode no good to us.   I am afraid we shall make but a poor business here.   Many families must be in mourning, and then, besides all these annoyances, the trouble which the police will give us."

"Bah !" cried I, "you take too dismal a view of everything."

We continued to talk about these strange events until long past midnight.   The fire in our little stove lighted up the angles of the roof, the square dormer window with its three cracked panes of glass, the mattress spread upon the bare boards, the blackened beams overhead, the little fir table, which cast an unsteady shadow on the worm-eaten floor.   A mouse, attracted by the heat, darted back and forth like an arrow along the wall.   We could hear the wind without, whistling and bellowing around the high chimney-stacks, sweeping the snow from the gutters beneath the eaves in misty swirls.   I was dreaming of Annette.   Silence had fallen upon us. Suddenly Wilfrid, throwing off his coat, cried :

" It is time to sleep ; put another stick of wood in the stove, and let us go to bed."

" Yes, that is the best thing we can do," said I, and began to pull off my boots. Two minutes afterward we were stretched on the mattress, the coverings drawn up to our chins, and a great log under our heads for a pillow. Wilfrid was asleep in a moment. The light from the little stove blazed up and died away, the wind redoubled its violence without, and, in the midst of dreams of Annette, I, too, in my turn, slept the sleep of the just.

About two o'clock in the morning I was awakened by a strange noise. At first I thought it was a cat running along the gutters ; but, my ear being close to the rafters, I could not remain long in doubt. Some one was walking over the roof. I touched Wilfrid with my elbow to awaken him.

" Hist !" whispered he, pressing my hand.

He also had heard the noise. The fire was just dying out, the last feeble flame flickered on the crumbling walls. I was on the point of springing from the bed, when, at a single blow, the little window, kept closed by a fragment of brick, was pushed open. A pale face, with red hair, eyes gleaming with phosphorescent light, and quivering cheeks appeared in the opening, and looked about the room. Our fright was so great that we could not utter a sound. The man passed first one leg, then the other, through the window, and descended into the garret so carefully that not a board creaked under his footsteps.

This man, with heavy, round shoulders, short and thick-set, his face wrinkled and set like a tiger couched to spring, was none other than the rider who had overtaken us on the road to Heidelberg. But what a change in his appearance since then! In spite of the excessive cold, he was in his shirt-sleeves, a pair of breeches belted about his waist, woollen stockings, and shoes with silver buckles. A long knife, flecked with blood, glittered in his hand.

Wilfrid and I gave ourselves up for lost. But he did not seem to see us under the shadow of the sloping roof, although the fire was fanned again into a blaze by the current of cold air from the open window. The intruder seated himself on a stool, cowering and shivering in a strange way. Suddenly his greenish-yellow eyes fixed themselves on me, his nostrils dilated; for more than a minute, which seemed to me an age, he stared at me. The blood stood still in my veins. Then at last, turning towards the fire, he coughed with a husky, hoarse sound, like that which a cat makes, without moving a muscle of his face. Drawing a watch from the fob of his pantaloons, he seemed to look at the hour, and then, whether from absence of mind or some other reason, I know not, laid it upon the table. At length, rising from his seat with an air of uncertainty, he looked towards the window, appeared for a moment to hesitate, and then passed out of the door, leaving it wide open behind him.

I jumped up to shove the bolt, but already the man's steps were creaking on the staircase two stories below. An irresistible curiosity overcame my terror. I heard a window open, which looked upon the court, and, in a moment, I was at the dormer in the landing of the stairs on the same side. The court, seen from this height, was like a deep well. A wall, fifty or sixty feet high, divided it into two parts. On the right was the court of a pork-butcher; on the left, that of the Pied-du-Mouton. The wall was covered with moss and the rank vegetation which flourishes in the shade. Its summit reached from the window which the marauder had just opened, in a straight line to the roof of a great, gloomy building in the rear of the Bergstrasse. All this I took in at a glance, as the moon shone out from among the heavy snow-laden clouds, and I trembled as I saw the man come out through the window, and fly along the top of this wall, his head bent forward, the long knife in his hand, while the wind whistled and wailed a dismal chorus.

He gained the roof in front, and disappeared through a window. I believed I must be dreaming. For several moments I remained with open mouth, my breast bare, and my hair blown about by the wind and wet by the sleet which fell from the eaves. At last, waking from my stupor, I returned to our garret, and found Wilfrid with face blanched, and haggard with fright, and muttering a prayer under his breath. I hastened to bolt the door, throw some wood into the stove, and slip on my clothes.

"Well?" asked my comrade, getting out of bed.

"Well," I replied, "we are safe this time. If that man did not see us, it was only because Heaven was not ready yet for us to die."

"Yes," he murmured, "yes; it is one of the assassins Annette told us about. Good Heavens! what a face! and what a knife!"

He fell back on the mattress. I swallowed

The Dean's Watch

what was left of the wine in the pitcher; and, as the fire was now burning brightly, filling the room with its heat, and the bolt seemed a strong one, I began to regain my courage.

Still, the watch was there; the man might return to look for it. Our fears awoke again at this idea.

"What is to be done now?" asked Wilfrid. "Our shortest plan will be to go back at once to the Black Forest. I have no wish to play any more double-bass. You can do as you choose——"

"But why? What should make us go back? We have committed no crime."

"Hush! speak low!" whispered he. "The word *crime* alone is enough to hang us if any one heard. Poor devils like us serve as examples for others. Were they only to find this watch here——"

"Come, Wilfrid," said I; "it is no use to lose one's head. I dare say, a crime has been committed this night in the neighbourhood, it is more than probable; but, instead of flying, an honest man should aid justice; he should——"

"But how aid it? how?"

"The simplest way will be to take the watch to-morrow to the provost, and tell him what has taken place."

15

"Never! never! I would not dare touch the watch."

"Very well; I will go myself. Come, let us go to bed again."

"No; I cannot sleep any more."

"As you will.—Light your pipe, then, and let us talk."

As soon as day dawned, I took the watch from the table. It was a very fine one, with two dials—one for the hours, the other for the minutes. Wilfrid seemed, however, by this time, to have regained his assurance.

"Kasper," he said, "all things considered, it will be better for me to go to the provost. You are too young for such a piece of business. You will not be able to explain properly."

"Just as you choose," I replied.

"Besides, it would seem strange for a man of my age to send a child."

"Oh, yes, Wilfrid; I understand."

I saw that his self-esteem had driven him to this resolution. He would have been ashamed to own to his comrades that he had shown less courage than I.

He took the watch, and we descended the stairs with grave faces. Passing through the alley which leads to the street Saint-Christophe, we heard the clinking of glasses and knives and forks. At the same time I recognised the voices of old Bremer and his two sons.

"Faith, Wilfrid," said I, "a good glass of wine would not be bad before we go out."

I pushed open the door into the saloon. All our friends were there; violins and horns hung upon the walls—the harp in one corner. They received us with joyful cries of welcome, and made us take seats at the table.

"Hey!" cried old Bremer; "good luck, comrades! See the snow, and the wind! The saloons will all be full. Every flake of snow in the air is a florin in our pockets!"

The sight of my little Annette, as fresh and piquant as ever, smiling on me with eyes and lips full of love, gave me new spirits. The best pieces of ham were for me; and, every time that she came to set down a glass near me, her hand would tenderly press my shoulder. Ah! how my heart beat, as I thought of the nuts which we had cracked together the night before!

Still, the pale face of the assassin would pass from time to time before my eyes, making me shudder at the recollection. I looked at Wilfrid. He was grave and thoughtful. As eight o'clock struck, we all rose to go, when suddenly the door opened, and three mean-looking fellows, with leaden faces, and eyes sharp as rats', followed by several more of the same sort, presented themselves on the threshold. One of them, with a long nose, which seemed to be on the scent for some mischief, a great cudgel in his fist, advanced with the demand—

"Your papers, gentlemen!"

Every one hastened to satisfy him. Unhappily, however, Wilfrid, who was standing near the stove, was seized with a sudden fit of trembling; and, as he saw the practised eye of the police agent regarding him with an equivocal look, the unlucky idea occurred to him of letting the watch slip down into his boot. Before it reached its destination, however, the officer stepped up to him, and, slapping him on the leg, cried, in a bantering tone:

"Ah! ha! something seems to trouble you here!"

Upon this, Wilfrid, to the consternation of all, succumbed entirely. He fell back upon a bench, as pale as death; and Madoc, the chief of police, with a malicious shout of laughter, drew forth the watch from his pantaloons. But, the moment the agent looked at it, he became grave.

"Let no one go out!" he thundered to his

The Dean's Watch

followers; "we've the whole gang here. 'Tis the watch of the dean, Daniel Van der Berg. Quick! the handcuffs!"

Thereupon arose a terrible tumult. Giving ourselves up for lost, I slipped down under the bench close to the wall. In spite of their protests, poor old Bremer, his sons, and Wilfrid, were all handcuffed. Just then I felt a soft little hand passed gently about my neck. It was Annette's, and I pressed my lips upon it as a last adieu, when, seizing my ear, she pulled it gently— gently. Under one end of the table I saw the cellar-door open; I slipped through; the trap-door closed.

All had passed in a second. In my hiding-place I heard them trampling over the door; then everything was still; my unlucky comrades were gone. Without, on the door-step, I heard Mother Grédel Dick lamenting in shrill tones the dishonour which had fallen on the Pied-du-Mouton.

All day long I remained squeezed behind a hogshead, with back bent and legs doubled under me—a prey to a thousand fears. Should a dog stray into the cellar—should the landlady take a fancy to refill the jug herself, or a fresh cask have to be broached—the least chance might be my destruction. I imagined old Bremer and his sons,

The Dean's Watch

Wilfrid, big Berthe herself, all hanging from the gibbet on the Harberg, in the middle of a great flock of crows that were feasting at their expense. My hair stood on end.

Annette, as anxious as myself, carefully closed the door each time she left the cellar.

"Leave the door alone," I heard the old woman say. "Are you a fool, to lose half your time in opening it?"

After that the door remained open. I saw the tables surrounded by new guests, who discussed in loud tones the doings of the famous band of murderers who had just been captured, and exulted over the fate in store for them. All the musicians from the Black Forest, they said, were bandits, who made a pretence of their trade to find their way into houses and spy out the bolts and bars, and then, next morning, the master would be found murdered in his bed, the mistress and children with their throats cut. They ought all to be exterminated without pity.

"All the town will go to see them hanged!" cried Mother Grédel. "It will be the happiest day of my life!"

"And to think that the watch of Maître Daniel was the means of their capture! He told the police of its loss, and gave them a description of it this morning; and, an hour afterward, Madoc bagged the whole covey."

Thereupon followed shouts of laughter and triumph. Shame, indignation, terror, made me hot and cold by turns.

Night came at last. All the drinkers had gone, save two or three who still lingered over their cups. A single candle remained lighted in the saloon.

"Go to bed, madame," said Annette's soft voice to Mother Grédel; "I will stay till these gentlemen go."

The carousers, tipsy as they were, understood the hint, and took their leave, one by one.

"At last," thought I, as I heard the last one go, stumbling and hiccoughing through the door —"they are all gone. Mother Grédel will go to bed. Annette will come, without delay, to deliver me."

In this agreeable anticipation, I had already disentangled my numb limbs, when these dreadful words of the portly landlady met my ears:

"Annette, go and close up, and do not forget the bar. I am going myself into the cellar."

Alas! this seemed to be the praiseworthy, but for me most unlucky, custom of the good lady—so as to see herself that all was right.

The Dean's Watch

"But, madame," stammered Annette, "there is no need; the cask is not empty——"

"Mind your own business," interrupted her mistress, whose candle already was shining at the top of the steps.

I had hardly time to crouch again behind the cask. The old woman went from one cask to the other, stooping beneath the low ceiling of the vault.

"Oh, the hussy!" I heard her mutter; "how she lets the wine leak out! But only wait—I will teach her to close the stopcocks better. Just to see! just to see!"

The light cast dark shadows on the walls glistening with moisture. I made myself as small as possible.

Suddenly, just as I thought the danger over, I heard a sigh from the stout dame—a sigh so long, so lugubrious, that it struck me at once. Something extraordinary must have happened. I risked a look. To my horror, I saw Mother Grédel, with open mouth, and eyes starting from her head, staring at the ground beneath the cask behind which I was standing motionless. She had espied one of my feet, projecting beneath the joist which supported the hogshead. No doubt, she thought she had discovered the chief of the brigands, hidden there for the purpose of cutting her throat during the night. My resolution was taken quickly. Rising up, I said in a low voice :

"Madame, for Heaven's sake, have pity on me ! I am——"

But thereupon, without listening—without even looking at me, she began to scream like any peacock—the shrillest, the most ear-piercing screams—and at the same time to clamber up the stairs as fast as her fat body would let her. Almost beside myself with terror, I clung to her robe—fell on my knees beside her. But this was worse still.

"Help ! help ! assassins ! murder !" she shrieked. "Oh ! oh ! Let me go ! Take my money ! Oh ! oh !"

It was frightful.

"Look at me, madame," I tried to say ; "I am not what you think."

But she was crazy with fear ; she raved, she gasped, she bawled at the top of her lungs—so that, had we not been underground, the whole quarter would have been aroused. In despair, and furious at her stupid folly, I clambered over her back, and gained the door before her—slammed it in her face, and shoved the bolt. During the struggle the light had been extinguished, and Mistress Grédel remained in the dark, her voice only faintly heard at intervals.

Exhausted, almost annihilated, I looked at Annette, whose distress was equal to mine. We stood listening in silence to the faint cries. Gradually they died away and ceased. The poor woman must have fainted.

"Oh, Kasper!" cried Annette, clasping her hands. "What is to be done? Fly! Save yourself! Have you killed her?"

"Killed her? I?"

"No matter—fly! Here—quick!"

And she drew the bar from before the street-door. I rushed into the street, without even thanking her—ungrateful wretch that I was! The night was black as ink—not a star to be seen, not a lamp lighted, snow driving before the wind. I ran on for half an hour, at least, before I stopped to take breath. I looked up—imagine my despair —there I was, right in front of the Pied-du-Mouton again. In my terror I had made the tour of the quarter perhaps two or three times, for aught I knew. My legs were like lead; my knees trembled.

The inn, just before deserted, was buzzing like a bee-hive. Lights went from window to window. It was full, no doubt, of police-agents. Exhausted with hunger and fatigue, desperate, not knowing where to find refuge, I took the most singular of all my resolutions.

"Faith," said I to myself, "one death as well as another! It is no worse to be hung than to leave one's bones on the road to the Black Forest. Here goes!"

And I entered the inn to deliver myself up to justice. Besides the shabby men with crushed hats and big sticks whom I had already seen in the morning, who were going and coming, and prying everywhere, before a table were seated the grand-provost Zimmer, dressed all in black, solemn, keen-eyed, and the secretary Rôth, with his red wig, imposing smile, and great, flat ears, like oyster-shells. They paid hardly any attention at all to me—a circumstance which at once modified my resolution. I took a seat in one corner of the hall, behind the great stove, in company with two or three of the neighbours, who had run in to see what was going on, and called calmly for a pint of wine and a plate of sauerkraut.

Annette came near betraying me.

"Ah, good Heavens!" she exclaimed; "is it possible that you are here?"

But luckily no one noticed her exclamation, and I ate my meal with better appetite, and listened to the examination of the good lady Grédel, who sat propped up in a big arm-chair, with hair dishevelled, and eyes still dilated by her fright.

" Of what age did this man seem to be ?" asked the provost.

" Forty or fifty, sir. It was an immense man, with black whiskers, or brown—I don't know exactly which—and a long nose, and green eyes."

" Had he no marks of any kind—scars, for instance ? "

" No, I can't remember. Luckily, I screamed so loud, he was frightened ; and then I defended myself with my nails. He had a great hammer and pistols. He seized me by the throat. Ah ! you know, sir, when one tries to murder you, you have to defend yourself."

" Nothing more natural, more legitimate, my dear madame.—Write, M. Rôth—' The courage and presence of mind of this excellent lady were truly admirable.' "

Then came Annette's turn, who simply declared that she had been so frightened she could remember nothing.

"This will do," said the provost. " If we need to make further inquiry, we will return to-morrow."

The Dean's Watch

The examination being thus ended, every one departed, and I asked Mme. Grédel to give me a room for the night. She did not in the least recollect ever having seen me before.

"Annette," she gasped, "take the gentleman to the little green room in the third story. As for myself, sir, you see I cannot even stand on my legs! O good Lord! good Lord! what does not one have to go through in this world!"

With this she fell to sobbing, which seemed to relieve her.

"Oh, Kasper, Kasper!" cried Annette, when she had taken me to my room, and we were alone, "who would have believed that you were one of the band? I can never, never forgive myself for having loved a brigand!"

"How? Annette, you too?" I exclaimed; "this is too much!"

"No, no!" she cried, throwing her arms about my neck, "you are not one of them—you are too good for that. Still, you are a brave man just the same to have come back."

I explained to her that I should have died of cold outside, and that this alone had decided me. After a few minutes, however, we parted so as not to arouse Mother Grédel's suspicions, and having made certain that none of the windows

27

opened on a wall, and that the bolt on the door was a good one, I went to bed and soon was fast asleep.

II

WHEN I drew the curtain of my bed next morning, I saw that the window-panes were white with snow, which was heaped up also on the sill without. I thought mournfully of my poor comrades' fate. How they must have suffered from cold! Old Bremer and big Berthe especially— my heart ached for them.

While I was absorbed in these sad reflections a strange noise arose outside. It drew near the inn, and, not without fear and trembling, I jumped out of bed and rushed to the window, to see what new danger threatened.

They were bringing the terrible band to confront it with Mme. Grédel Dick. My poor companions came down the street between two files of policemen, and followed by a perfect avalanche of ragamuffins, yelling and hissing like true savages. There was poor Bremer, handcuffed to his son Ludwig, then Carl and Wilfrid, and last of all stout Berthe, who walked by herself, lamenting her fate all the while in heart-rending tones :

The Dean's Watch

" For Heaven's sake, gentlemen, for Heaven's sake, have pity on a poor innocent harpist! I—kill! I—rob! Oh! good Lord! can it be possible?"

And she wrung her hands. The others looked doleful enough as they walked with heads bent, and dishevelled hair hanging over their faces.

The procession, rabble and all, turned into the dark alley which led to the inn. Presently the guards drove out the eager crowd, who remained outside in the mud, with their noses flattened against the window-panes.

I dressed myself quickly, and opened my door, to see if there were not some chance of escape, but I could hear voices and footsteps going to and fro down-stairs, and made up my mind that the passages were well guarded. My door opened on the landing, just opposite the window which our midnight visitor of the night before must have used in his flight. At first I paid no attention to this window, but, while I remained listening, on a sudden I perceived that it was open—that there was but little snow on the sill, and drawing near I perceived that there were fresh tracks along the wall. I shuddered at this discovery. The man had been there again, perhaps he came every night. The cat, the weasel, the ferret, all such beasts of prey, have their accustomed paths in this way. In a moment, everything was clear to my mind.

"Ah," thought I, "if chance has thus put the assassin's fate in my hands, my poor comrades may be saved."

Just at this moment the door of the saloon was opened, and I could hear some words of the examination going on.

"Do you admit having participated, on the 20th of this month, in the assassination of the priest Ulmet Elias?"

Then followed some words which I could not make out, and the door was closed again. I leaned my head on the banister, debating in my mind a great, an heroic resolution. "Heaven has put the fate of my companions in my hands. I can save them. If I recoil from such a duty, I shall be their murderer! my peace of mind, my honour, will be gone forever! I shall feel myself the most contemptible of men!"

For a long time I hesitated, but all at once my resolution was taken. I descended the stairs and made my way into the hall.

"Have you never seen this watch?" the provost was saying to Grédel. "Try to recollect, madame."

The Dean's Watch

Without awaiting her answer, I advanced and replied myself, in a firm voice : "This watch, sir, I have seen in the hands of the assassin himself, I recognise it, and I can deliver the assassin into your hands this very night, if you will but listen to me."

Profound silence for a moment followed my address. The astounded officials looked at each other ; my comrades seemed to revive a little.

"Who are you, sir?" demanded the provost, recovering himself.

"I am the comrade of these unfortunate men, and I am not ashamed to own it," I cried, "for all, all of them, though poor, are honest. Not one of them is capable of committing the crime they are accused of."

Once more there was silence. The great Berthe began to sob under her breath. The provost seemed to reflect. At last, looking at me sternly, he said :

"Where do you pretend you will find the assassin for us?"

"Here, sir, in this house, and, to convince you, I only ask to speak one moment to you in private."

"Come," said he, rising.

He motioned to the chief detective, Madoc, to follow us, and we went out.

The Dean's Watch

I ran quickly up-stairs; the others close behind me. On the third story, I stopped before the window, and pointed out the tracks in the snow.

"There are the assassin's footsteps," said I. "This is where he passes every evening. Night before last he came at two o'clock in the morning. Last night he was here; no doubt he will return to-night."

The provost and Madoc looked at the footsteps for several moments without saying a word.

"And how do you know these are the footprints of the murderer?" asked the chief of police, incredulously.

I told them about the man's entrance into our garret, and pointed out above us the lattice through which I had watched his flight in the moonlight. "It was only by accident," I said, "that I had discovered the footsteps this morning."

"Strange!" muttered the provost. "This modifies considerably the position of the prisoners. But how do you explain the murderer's being in the cellar?"

"The murderer was myself, sir."

And I related in a few words the events of the night before.

The Dean's Watch

"That will do," said he, and then, turning to the chief of police, continued:

"I must confess, Madoc, that these fiddlers' story has seemed to me by no means conclusive of their having had anything to do with the murders. Besides, their papers establish, for several of them, an *alibi* very hard to disprove.—Still, young man, though the account you give us has the appearance of being true, you will remain in our power until it is verified.—Madoc, do not lose sight of him, and take your measures accordingly."

With this he went down-stairs, collected his papers, and ordered the prisoners to be taken back to jail. Then, casting a look of contempt at the corpulent landlady, he took his departure, followed by his secretary.

"Madame," said Madoc, who remained with two of his men, "you will please preserve the most profound silence as to what has taken place. Also, prepare for this brave lad here the same room he occupied night before last."

His tone admitted of no reply, and Mme. Grédel promised by all that was sacred to do whatever they wished, if they would only save her from the brigands.

"Give yourself no uneasiness about the brigands," replied Madoc. "We will stay here all

day and all night to protect you. Go quietly about
your affairs, and begin by giving us breakfast.—
Young man, will you do me the honour to breakfast with me?"

My situation did not permit me to decline this
offer. I accepted.

We were soon seated in front of a ham and a
bottle of Rhine wine. The chief of police, in
spite of his leaden face—his keen eye and great
nose like the beak of an eagle—was a jolly enough
fellow after a few glasses of wine. He tried to
seize Annette by the waist as she passed. He told
funny stories, at which the others shouted with
laughter. I, however, remained silent, depressed.

"Come, young man," said Madoc, with a laugh,
"try to forget the death of your estimable grandmother. We are all mortal. Take a good drink,
and chase away all these gloomy thoughts."

So the time slipped away, amid clouds of
tobacco-smoke, the jingling of glasses, and clinking of cans. We sat apart during the day in one
corner of the saloon. Guests came to drink as
usual, but they paid no attention to us. At nine
o'clock, however, after the watchman had gone his
round, Madoc rose.

"Now," said he, "we must attend to our little
business. Close the door and shutters—softly,

madame, softly. There, you and Mlle. Annette may go to bed."

The chief and his two followers drew from their pockets bars of iron loaded at the ends with leaden balls. Madoc put a fresh cap on his pistol, and placed it carefully in the breast-pocket of his overcoat, so as to be ready at hand.

Then we mounted to the garret. The too-attentive Annette had lighted a fire in the stove. Madoc, muttering an oath between his teeth, hastened to throw some water on the coals. Then he pointed to the mattress.

" If you have any mind for it," said he to me, "you can sleep."

He blew out the candle, and seated himself with his two acolytes in the back part of the room against the wall. I threw myself on the bed, murmuring a prayer that Heaven would send the assassin.

The hours rolled by. Midnight came. The silence was so profound I could scarcely believe the three men sat there with eye and ear strained to catch the least movement—the slightest sound. Minute after minute passed slowly—slowly. I could not sleep. A thousand terrible images chased each other through my brain. One o'clock struck—two—yet nothing—no one appeared.

The Dean's Watch

At three o'clock one of the policemen moved. I thought the man was coming—but all was silent again as before. I began to think that Madoc would take me for an impostor, to imagine how he would abuse me in the morning. And then my poor comrades, instead of aiding, I had only riveted their chains!

The time seemed now to pass only too rapidly. I wished the night might last forever, so as to preserve at least a ray of hope for me.

I was going over the same torturing fancies for the hundredth time—on a sudden, without my having heard the least sound—the window opened—two eyes gleamed in the aperture—nothing moved in the garret.

"They have gone to sleep!" thought I, in an agony of suspense.

The head remained there—motionless—watchful. The villain must suspect something! Oh! how my heart thumped—the blood coursed through my veins! And yet cold beads of sweat gathered on my forehead. I ceased to breathe.

Several minutes passed thus—then, suddenly, the man seemed to have decided—he glided down into the garret, with the same noiseless caution as on the previous night.

The Dean's Watch

But at the same instant a cry—a terrible, short, thrilling cry—vibrated through the room.

"We have him!"

Then the whole house was shaken from garret to cellar by cries—the stamping of feet—hoarse shouts. I was petrified by terror. The man bellowed—the others drew their breaths in quick gasps—then came a heavy fall which made the floor crack—and I heard only the gnashing of teeth and clink of chains.

"Light!" cried the terrible Madoc.

By the flame of the burning coals, which cast a bluish light through the room, I could dimly see the police-officers crouched over the body of a man in his shirt-sleeves; one held him by the throat, the knees of the other rested upon his chest; Madoc was roughly clasping the handcuffs on his wrists. The man lay as if lifeless, save that from time to time one of his great legs, naked from knee to ankle, was raised and struck the floor with a convulsive movement. His eyes were starting from their sockets—a blood-stained foam had gathered upon his lips.

Hardly had I lighted the candle when the officers started back with an exclamation:

"Our dean!"

The Dean's Watch

And all three rose to their feet, looking at each other with pale faces.

The bloodshot eye of the assassin turned towards Madoc, his lips moved, but only after several seconds I could hear him murmur :

"What a dream !— Good God ! what a dream !"

Then a sigh, and he lay motionless again.

I drew near to look at him. Yes, it was he, the man who had overtaken us on the road to Heidelberg, and advised us to turn back. Perhaps even then he had a presentiment that we would be the cause of his ruin. Madoc, who had recovered from his surprise, seeing that he did not move, and that a thread of blood was oozing along the dusty floor, bent over him and tore asunder the bosom of his shirt ; he had stabbed himself to the heart with his huge knife.

"Eh !" said Madoc, with a sinister smile. "Monsieur the dean has cheated the gallows. He knew where to strike, and has not missed his mark. Do you stay here," he continued to us. "I will go and inform the provost."

I remained with the two police agents, watching the corpse.

By eight o'clock next morning all Heidelberg was electrified with the news. Daniel Van der

The Dean's Watch

Berg, dean of the woollen-drapers, possessed of wealth and position such as few enjoyed, who could believe that he had been the terrible assassin?

A hundred different explanations were offered. Some said the rich dean had been a somnambulist, and therefore not responsible for his actions—others, that he had murdered from pure love of blood—he could have had no other motive for such a crime. Perhaps both theories were true. In the somnambulist the will is dead, he is governed by his animal instincts alone, be they pacific or sanguinary, and in Master Daniel Van der Berg, the cruel face, the flat head swollen behind the ears—the green eyes—the long bristling mustache, all proved that he unhappily belonged to the feline family—terrible race, which kills for the pleasure of killing.

THE END OF THE DEAN'S WATCH

THE PORTRAITS OF
ERCKMANN AND CHATRIAN

ÉMILE ERCKMANN.
After a portrait by Otto de
Frère, about 1856.

THE popular names of Erckmann-Chatrian, names which recall so many stirring and patriotic tales, represent, to our great regret, only a very obscure and unæsthetic iconography. We have but very few pictures of the authors of *Madame Thérèse* and *L'Ami Fritz*. Simple and rural in their tastes, Erckmann and Chatrian, without at any time parading that celebrity in which so many authors of "smart" literature take so much pride, when in the most brilliant epoch of their fame still preserved that rustic simplicity which characterized their first appearance. With their genial and upright natures these two Alsatians never thought to put themselves before their works. They were men of a bygone age, Nature's philosophers, wise men without vanity. Our task in respect of them has been difficult, but we hope not altogether infelicitous. It is not without a certain satisfaction that, by the side of other personalities so often popularized, we have been able by dint of persevering research to discover two or three portraits of these writers.

Thus we have given as frontispiece two pictures of these Siamese twins of literature, ingenuously painted, in timid and awkward strokes, by one of those travelling professors of the familiar art of charcoal and pencil, such as were to be seen in the villages of Alsace about fifty years ago. It portrays the "Amis Fritz" and the worthy pastors seated round the tables in the old Gothic inns.

A detached portrait of Erckmann by Otto de Frère, of about the year 1864 or 1865, gives us an opportunity of studying more closely one of the collaborators. Émile Erckmann, born in 1822, at Phalsbourg, has in the portrait before us already passed his fortieth year. The calm features and high bald forehead of the professor leave an impression of gravity and thoughtfulness. A pair of spectacles which he wears adds to his pedagogical appearance. Émile Erckmann represents the philosophic and the contemplative side of this romantic couple. Born in a town which has given so many

Erckmann and Chatrian

chiefs to the French army, he brought to their joint work a deep and profound study of the Alsatian land, together with the silent tenacity of his race. The confined life of his province, rural and industrious in times of peace, implacable and ardent in the hour of strife, finds in him an able and truthful historian.

The first portrait of Émile Erckmann is contemporary with *Madame Thérèse*, one of the most admirable and best known of their *romans nationaux*. A second portrait, which is reproduced here, seems a trifle older and of about the year 1868.

ERCKMANN
About 1868.

That year the Théâtre de Cluny in Paris produced a piece adapted by the two friends from the novel *Le Juif Polonais*. Erckmann at that time wore a beard. His dress, like his appearance, is without care, but in that serious face and behind those spectacles there shines the profound and concentrated look of one accustomed to gaze upon the waters and the mountains of the Vosges; and the expression, brilliant as a fixed star, obliterates all that is crude and inharmonious in this face, which otherwise reminds one of a German schoolmaster. In contradistinction to Chatrian, who spent nearly the whole of his life in Paris and its environs, Erckmann seems to pine for the green woods and scenery of that beautiful country where the healthy and simple people are so much in harmony with nature. Thus is he shown to us here. His features remind us both of Taine and Cherbuliez, though he possessed nothing in common with them beyond that serene look full of reflection and deduction. Erckmann worked in Alsace; Chatrian, on the contrary, whose administrative duties kept him all day at his desk in Paris, could indulge his taste for novel-writing only in the evenings, occasionally stealing a few hours in the day out of the time which he was bound to devote to his Government work. To the calm and quietude of his companion Chatrian added the animation of an ardent and inventive spirit. To the reflective and poetic talent of Erckmann, he opposed the hastiness of his own dashing and spontaneous genius. To his pen, no doubt, can be assigned all those parts where the story, leaving the description of rustic life, plunges boldly into dramatic action.

A double portrait, from a photograph taken about 1874, depicts them in the constrained attitude characteristic of the work of Daguerre and his followers. Doubtless they were together in that little house at Raincy, where they often met to discuss the plot of some new work, and where the photographer must have invaded their privacy.

"Only once did I see that little garden at Raincy," writes one of their friends, "but I can

ERCKMANN AND CHATRIAN
About 1874. (After a photograph.)

see again the kindly, portly Erckmann seated under the shade of a cherry-tree, a picture which later on I saw reproduced again at the Théâtre Français in *L'Ami Fritz*—Erckmann with his calm face and shrewd eyes, smoking his pipe, and throwing out philosophical theories between the whiffs of tobacco. He is, as it were, the dream, and Chatrian the reality in this partnership. Erckmann would willingly have kept to the fantastic tales of their early days, but it was Chatrian, the type of the soldier, with the mustache and face of a somewhat harsh-looking non-commissioned officer, and a strict disciplinarian, who directed the collaboration towards the Napoleonic era and the national chronicles. This, in a measure, explains the portraits and helps us to show them both, united in a work simultaneously conceived, both simple and great in their baffling expression, happy in knowing themselves understood by the multitude of the poor and humble. That photograph dates from the representation of *L'Ami Fritz* in the Théâtre Français.

After the defeat of the Alsatians these poets, deeply touched, sing to us in their heartfelt words of the picturesqueness of their mountains and forests, henceforth to be under Cerman rule. At that moment (and it is also the last portrait we have been able to find) Erckmann is aged, his beard and mustache are silvered, his appearance no longer that of a professor, but rather that of an old officer whom the close of the war has thrown out of employment. Chatrian, on the other hand, though only four years his junior, with hair and beard still abundant, seems alive with vigour and strength. His glance is keen, frank, and loyal, his

face open and bold, his attitude full of energy.
No picture could express better than this the
striking contrast between two temperaments so
widely dissimilar, and yet so well designed to sup-
plement each other and form a complete whole.

André Gill, in a typical and humorous caricature, has admirably shown the expressions of the
two writers as their faces appear above a jug of

ERCKMANN AND CHATRIAN.
After a caricature by André Gill, 1879.

beer, each with an Alsatian pipe in his mouth. A
peaceful happiness marks th ir brotherly features.
They are enjoying the dramatic successes of the
Rantzau and *Madame Thérèse*. The final dis-
agreement, which did not happen until 1890, at
Villemomble, and which ended only with Cha-

trian's death, had not yet come, like a detestable intruder, to separate those two strong characters. Their dreams, their work, and their successes were still joint property at the time André Gill drew this caricature. The two writers have been termed the "Siamese twins" of historical romance. One cannot understand why these two figures, so full of contrast, were never delineated in painting nor sculpture, in view of the large measure of success which directed attention to their names. Such incomprehensible mysteries do sometimes occur in the lives of celebrated men, and we fail to find the solution of the enigma, which forces us to admit that Erckmann and Chatrian left us no portraits, no important engravings, no great popular lithographs, nor any medallions or busts. If ever posterity thinks of raising a monument to the memory of these two curious writers, the artist to whom the task is assigned will have some difficulty in finding any other valid and interesting documents than the few pictures which are collected here.

OCTAVE UZANNE.

THE END